When the down and out
Australian country town
that they would stay for long; nor, when they left, that it
would be without their daughter Lilli.

It was a mystery, too, why wealthy Miss Dalgleish
should 'buy' the wilful girl and try to tame her, for
though she accepted food, clothes and education as part
of her grooming, Lilli was fiercely determined never to
be anyone but Lilli.

With a battle of wills for possession of her soul, and with
the unexpected return of her scavenging family, what
did the real future hold for Lilli?

**Also by James Aldridge**

*Signed With Their Honour*
*The Sea Eagle*
*Of Many Men*
*The Diplomat*
*The Hunter*
*Heroes Of The Empty View*
*I Wish He Would Not Die*
*The Last Exile*
*A Captive In The Land*
*The Stateman's Game*
*My Brother, Tom*
*A Sporting Proposition*
*The Marvellous Mongolian*
*Mockery In Arms*
*The Untouchable Juli*
*One Last Glimpse*
*Goodbye Un-America*
*The Broken Saddle*

Short Stories

*Gold And Sand*

Non-fiction

*Cairo*
*Living Egypt* (with Paul Strand)

# THE TRUE STORY OF LILLI STUBECK

James Aldridge

**Puffin Books**

Puffin Books
Penguin Books Australia Ltd,
487 Maroondah Highway, P.O. Box 257
Ringwood, Victoria, 3134, Australia
Penguin Books Ltd,
Harmondsworth, Middlesex, England
Penguin Books,
40 West 23rd Street, New York, N.Y. 10010, U.S.A.
Penguin Books Canada Ltd,
2801 John Street, Markham, Ontario, Canada, L3R 1B4
Penguin Books (N.Z.) Ltd,
182-190 Wairau Road, Auckland 10, New Zealand

First published 1984 by Hyland House Publishing Pty Ltd, Melbourne
Published in Puffin, 1985
Reprinted 1985

Offset from the Hyland House edition.
Made and printed in Australia by
The Dominion Press–Hedges & Bell

**CIP**

Aldridge, James, 1918–
The true story of Lilli Stubeck.

ISBN 0 14 032055 5.

I. Title.

A823'.3

If there ever was a Lilli Stubeck,
this would be her true story as far as
I am able to tell it.

# 1

MOST PEOPLE IN OUR TOWN THOUGHT LILLI STUBECK 'A WICKED little thing' when she was a child and then at the end they said with a shake of the head that she was 'a tragedy'. And though 'tragedy' in our town represented anything from a lost opportunity to a misconception or an illegitimacy (not Lilli's problem) it was said as if her curious fate was something she thoroughly deserved.

I never thought that way myself, not because I had better standards to go by but because I knew Lilli better than most people and at the end of it all I had more information than anybody else.

The Stubecks arrived in our country town of St Helen like a load of chopped wood: eight children on an old cart drawn by a horse so thin and shaggy and scaled with hard mud that it looked like something pre-historic. My mother told me they had come into the town as gypsies, but they were not real gypsies, even though they were all nut-brown and cheeky-eyed and curly-haired. But there was something foreign about them, as if they had brought something with them from another country. Even some of their expressions were not truly Australian.

They had moved into a deserted house on a bend in the Murray River which we called The Point because it was a little peninsula all to itself, with willow trees along the banks and large gum trees and dead and dying peach and almond trees around the low-roofed house. The house belonged to an old woman named Mrs Carson who lived like a hermit in a nearby town, and for ten years before the Stubecks arrived no one had lived in the house except tramps and seasonal fruit pickers and other itinerants who had gradually wrecked it, burning most of its window frames and doors and some of the flooring for heat and cooking fuel. It was always overrun with mice.

Within a few days of their arrival the Stubeck children (four sons and four daughters) had been seen all over the town as if inspecting it thoroughly for loot, because they quickly established themselves as thieves, scavengers and beggars. Matty Stubeck was a little nut of a man, aggressive, quick-witted, scheming, begging and obsequious or cheeky depending on what he was after. He was half the size of his silent dark-eyed wife who was powerful enough to pick up her husband and shake him, which she did from time to time, although Matty didn't lose any authority or stature in his family as a result. He was like a weasel in all things, particularly the darting nips and blows which his children (even his teenage sons) had to suffer any time that Matty felt like hitting out at somebody. On the other hand Mrs Stubeck rarely hit the children, as if there was some rule in the household that it was the man's duty to do the talking and the chastising. In fact all the girls were silent and rarely spoke. Mrs Stubeck was not bright, but her sudden grip on an arm or a shoulder or a neck was more feared than Matty's unexpected and whiplike slaps.

It was always a mystery to the town how they lived. In Australia we were in the middle of the great depression of the thirties and work was scarce, in fact almost non-existent for itinerants like Matty except some fruit-picking in season. Yet the family survived in dark, ruddy health. They were never ill, though they wore threadbare clothes in summer and winter and lived in a draughty, crowded two-roomed house. The four boys were most often seen scavenging at the back of the shops, the hotels, the butter factory, the slaughter yards, or somewhere in the vicinity of the railway station and goods yards. Even if there had been work we knew the Stubecks wouldn't have bothered. At most Matty would sometimes offer a load of wood around the town (we cooked then on wood stoves).

When he asked my father one day if he wanted a load cheap, my father said: 'I'll take it if you cut some of it in half.'

'Not me,' Matty said.

The Stubecks would gather dead wood from along the river, but they wouldn't put an axe to it. Though they lived on the river they were poor fishermen, and they would steal the catch from any of the crayfish nets we put down. In fact The Point was a good place for crayfish but we never put down our nets there (wire drums, really) because we knew that Matty would steal anything in them. And whenever we put down a net elsewhere in the river we tried to hide all evidence of it so that the Stubecks couldn't find it.

Yet Matty had one craft which surprised us and made people wonder where he might have come from in the first place. Whenever he gathered wood in the bush he would often steal some fencing wire from the remote corner of a mallee farm, and with a little hand-forge he would heat the wire and plait it into startling patterns to fit the wire-screen doors and windows that most houses had. They were such pure decoration, however, that he had a hard time selling them in those difficult times.

'How much do you want for it, Stubeck?' my father once asked Matty when he stood at our back door with a curiously distorted design which might have filled one of the panels of our screen door.

'You tell me what you want to pay for it,' Matty replied.

'Two shillings,' my father said.

'Not on your life,' Matty told him. 'It's worth a lot more than that, and you know it.'

'The wire is stolen and the workmanship is poor,' my father pointed out, although the workmanship was excellent and he knew it.

'You're not getting it for two shillings.'

'All right. Three.'

'You've got the wrong man, Mr Quayle,' Matty said. 'It's well made and I bought the wire at Harding's only two days ago. Anyway I didn't think you would buy anything that was stolen, so why are you offering me two shillings?'

My father was a hot-tempered Englishman and a lawyer whose fanatical honesty was well-known in the town, but having been trapped so easily into a specious piece of bargaining he sent Matty packing, insisting that he never intended to buy it in the first place.

'That's what you say,' Matty shouted from the safety of the gate.

At the time of their arrival Lilli Stubeck was the youngest in the family. She was then seven. But a few months later another Stubeck was born, a tiny boy with only three fingers on both his hands, and my own memory of little Jackie as he grew older is of those three fingers clinging desperately to Lilli whenever I saw them together. I rarely saw him with his mother, and Lilli seemed unaware that she was carrying him on her hip, though she was hardly big enough to lift him.

Even so, Lilli was not a 'little mother'. She was the quickest and brightest of the four girls (the other three were Grace, Alice and Pansy) and, even more vivid than the picture of little Jackie clinging to her, I remember Lilli then as a silent alley-cat with an alley-cat's almond eyes who could appear from nowhere and disappear again in the same way, but always carrying a sugarbag which had something in it—something filched or picked up or acquired, though only once (much later) did I ever discover what she did have in it.

Lilli's arrival at our country school was something of an event because she was brought into class by the local police sergeant long after the school year had commenced. None of the Stubeck children had been sent to school on opening day and Sergeant Collins had called on them about a month later and forcibly brought two of the girls and one of the boys to school, the rest claiming to be more than fourteen, which was the school leaving age then.

Lilli stood at the door of the classroom looking like a small Rusalka plucked from dark, green water. Her faded cotton dress barely covered her lithe brown body. She wore no shoes, which wasn't unusual for boys (I didn't wear any myself) but girls usually wore something. In fact Lilli's bare legs and feet always had a curious abandon about them. Later I would realise that Lilli not only had little sense of propriety, she had none at all of body.

'In you go, you little devil,' Sergeant Collins said to her. He gave her a little push and left her.

Lilli moved a few inches, shook her shoulders and stared boldly at the mixed class of boys and girls. We stared back, and Lilli suddenly screwed up her face, hooked her hands into claws, showed her teeth and made a hissing noise like a fighting cat.

We all laughed.

'That's enough.' Our schoolmistress, Miss MacGill, was a shapeless middle-aged spinster with short, grey, bobbed hair and a deep voice which had earned her the nickname 'Boom'. She was an excellent teacher and a just one, and without sentiment of any kind. 'Come forward,' she boomed at Lilli.

Lilli remained where she was, and one of the favoured boys of the class called out, 'She's a gypsy, Miss, and doesn't understand English.'

'It's none of your business Andrew Allen what she is, so be quiet,' Miss MacGill said, and gripping Lilli firmly by the arm she led her to a desk where the happiest girl in the class was sitting—Dorothy Malone. 'Tomorrow,' Miss MacGill told her, 'you must bring a copybook, a pencil, a rubber, and no excuses. The one thing I won't have is excuses.'

Lilli said nothing, but she sat throughout the lesson watching the rest of us as if deciding one by one what she would do to us when she got the chance. At the first recess she leapt on Andrew Allen and tore the buttons off his shirt as she tried to pull him over.

'You wait,' she said. 'You just wait.'

The next day Lilli failed to turn up at school and once again Sergeant Collins was sent to bring her. This time Matty was threatened with prosecution, so he gave Lilli a quick, hard slap across the back of the neck and ordered her to school. She had no copybook, pencil or rubber but, as if anticipating the inevitable, Dorothy Malone silently produced a spare copybook, pencil and rubber from her school bag. Dorothy was the daughter of the town's prosperous Chevrolet and Marmon concessionaire, and Lilli accepted the gift the way she accepted all offerings. In fact it would remain an aspect of the lasting friendship of these two girls that the quiet and happy Dorothy would often anticipate some urgent need of Lilli's, and Lilli would accept it all as perfectly natural.

'Lilli,' Miss MacGill said to her. 'Since you seem to

enjoy behaving like a cat you can begin your lessons by writing out the words "I am not a cat".' Miss MacGill wrote the sentence on the blackboard for Lilli to copy.

Ten minutes later Lilli had not written a word and Miss MacGill stood over her for a moment, thinking. Miss MacGill knew all about laughter and ridicule because she had suffered so much of it herself. She also knew how to use it.

'I didn't realise that you can't write yet, Lilli,' she said, 'so take your copybook and go next door to the infants' class where Miss Singelton will teach you the alphabet.'

We laughed. Miss MacGill knew we would.

Lilli hesitated a moment, looked at Boom as if planning a later retaliation, and began to scratch her way through 'I am not a cat', which was, I suppose, the first step in an education that would become a very curious and complicated one for Lilli.

In the recess she chased the three or four boys and girls who had miaowed at her and called her 'Kitty-cat', and those she caught didn't repeat it. The strange thing is that the very girls who mocked her and sometimes took their punishment for it were often the same girls who tried hardest to be friends with Lilli.

My own brush with Lilli established a friendship that would last until the very last day I saw her. She came to our house one Saturday morning with her mother. I was doing my Saturday chores, digging little canals around my mother's rose bushes, when my mother called out to me:

'Kit. Someone's knocking at the front door. Go around and tell them for heaven's sake to come to the back. I don't want to bother with the front door now.'

Anybody in the town who was coming to our house at this time of a Saturday morning would know better than to go to the front door, so I wondered who it was. I was about nine at the time and I pictured some mysterious uncle from England suddenly arriving to surprise us with his pockets full of gold. But it was Mrs Stubeck, wrapped in a stained, voluminous skirt and holding a tattered wicker basket. Lilli was standing beside her carrying little Jackie on her hip and a sugarbag on her arm. Lilli and the baby were grubby from head to foot.

'Which one are you?' Mrs Stubeck said to me.

'Kit,' I said. 'But you'll have to go around the back Mrs Stubeck. You won't get any answer here.'

I led the way to the back door and called out: 'It's Mrs Stubeck.' I knew my mother was saying to herself: 'What on earth does she want?'

'Hello Mrs Quayle,' Mrs Stubeck said when my mother appeared at the back door. 'Do you want any washing or scrubbing done? Any cleaning or shifting?'

My mother closed the wire door firmly behind her and said, 'No thank you, Mrs Stubeck. I haven't got anything for you.'

'You've got a big house, Mrs Quayle. You must have something that needs doing. I'll beat your rugs for a shilling.'

'They don't need beating, thank you,' my mother said, knowing that the Stubecks only asked for work if they had something else in mind.

'Then your stove needs blacking,' Mrs Stubeck informed my mother and I knew that it was now a contest of temperament between an aggressive Mrs Stubeck and a defensive Mrs Quayle. My mother was far too gentle to stand up to this kind of attack and Mrs Stubeck was now pushing her way into the house.

'I've got nothing for you,' my mother said desperately, holding her back.

'Let me see,' Mrs Stubeck insisted, her hand on the doorknob.

'Kit,' my mother called in a panic. 'Go and get your father. He's next door.'

My father was a mile away in his office in the middle of the town but I knew what was happening, so to make a pretence of calling him from next door I ran across the vegetable patch to our back gate, then ran around the outside to the front gate and by the time I was back Mrs Stubeck was gone.

'They're in the garden,' my mother said to me.

Our large garden was filled with orange trees, plums,

apricots, passionfruit, peaches, grapes and vegetables, and my father had the first nectarine tree in our town — given him by the local citrus inspector whom he had helped in a legal quarrel with a citrus grower. The tree was about to bear its first ripe fruit, and I found Lilli Stubeck stripping it of its dozen, beautiful, ripening jewels. She had put the baby on the ground near her and she was filling her sugarbag with the fruit.

Aghast, I said 'What did you do that for?'

Lilli took the last nectarine from the tree and gave it to baby Jackie. 'You've got plenty more,' she said and pointed to a laden peach tree nearby.

'They're peaches,' I said. 'You've taken all the nectarines.' My father had forbidden anyone to touch the fruit; they were going to be a special treat.

I tried to take the sugarbag from Lilli, but she was a fighter, a scratcher and a girl, and she simply pushed me over. 'Don't be silly,' was all she said, and she moved over to the peach tree and began to strip that as well.

'Kit. Where are you?' I heard my mother call.

'Here,' I said and ran around the side of the house to join her.

'Look what she's doing,' my mother said.

Mrs Stubeck was on the other side of the garden stripping a plum tree, filling the sugarbag and ignoring my mother.

'We'll pay you for everything Missus,' Mrs Stubeck said as my mother stood there, helpless and non-violent.

I too was non-violent, but I suppose I had some faint family pride, or rather I didn't like to see my mother so helpless. There was a hose attached to a tap near the peach tree and I ran around the house again, turned on the tap and pointed the hose at Lilli who was up the peach tree sitting on a bough.

'Oh my gawd!' she cried as I soaked her.

I kept the hose on her as she came down the tree. Holding her hands out in defence, she pushed her way against the stream and tried to pull the hose out of my grasp. I didn't give it up but she managed to turn it on me. Inevitably baby Jackie, who was still sitting in the dirt, was also soaked, and he began to scream. Lilli was swearing and kicking at me as I tried to push her away, and when her mother arrived I had almost succeeded. In fact I managed to soak Mrs Stubeck as well.

'You little devil,' she said and cuffed me hard.

I knew when I was beaten so I took to my heels and ran up the ramp to the back door. In the meantime my mother had decided to act, which meant that she was now looking for Mrs Stubeck with the only weapon available—a whisk broom.

It ended in a Stubeck retreat. Lilli was soaked and muddy and angry. Still holding the baby and the bag of nectarines she shouted at me as she left, 'I'll get you for this, Kit Quayle.'

It was the sort of things that boys usually shouted in retreat, not girls. But I kept quiet because I knew Lilli meant it.

When my father came home he was furious about the nectarines and he told my mother he intended bringing the Stubecks to court. But my mother said, 'What on earth for?'

'Robbery with violence,' my father replied.

My mother talked him out of it. 'What sort of punishment would you want? Recompense? Prison for Mrs Stubeck? Kit did the right thing with the hose. They won't come back again,' she said. 'So if I were you I should forget it.'

That was not likely as far as my father was concerned, and though I don't remember exactly how he did it I know that he not only warned Mrs Stubeck never to come near our house again, but on principle he somehow did extract two shillings from them in payment for the stolen fruit.

As for Lilli: twice she chased me barefoot around the school grounds yelling threats, and because she was a girl I ran rather than confront her. She did manage to catch me the third time, but I was strong enough to hold her tough little arms and argue with her.

'We're quits,' I said.

'No we're not,' she said. 'You squirted me.'

'You got all our nectarines,' I pointed out.

Lilli thought for a moment and said: 'All right. Let me go.'

I released her arms. She kicked me on the shins with a bare foot and said: 'Now we're quits.'

We stood looking at each other for a moment, sizing up each other's character and the long future before us. I think Lilli knew that I was not a mocker and never would be. I hated it as much as she did. So we parted as equals, which was as far as you could go with Lilli.

# 2

BETWEEN THAT FIRST YEAR AND THE TIME WHEN THE RICHEST
and most cultured woman in town, Miss Dalgleish, acquired
Lilli, she went on establishing her reputation among us as
a wicked little thing, although almost all of it was based on
her simple philosophy of easy acquisition, and retaliation
for any slight she suffered. But Lilli always made a strict
differentiation between herself and her family. You could
insult her sisters or even make disparaging remarks about
her parents and she didn't seem to hear them.

In fact there was even a curious distinction in the share
of the family spoils, which allowed certain loot to be
common property and other acquisitions to be personal.
Food was always shared in common, so was money—the
little they saw of it. Buttermilk from the butter factory, for
instance, could not be touched until it was in the house.
'Spoiled butter' (yoghurt, really, which is probably one of
the reasons why they were so healthy) was a luxury they
always shared. But soft windfalls were never shared. I
once saw Lilli unearth a box of rock-hard snowballs (a
meringue-like mixture) discarded in the dustbin by the
sweet shop a few doors away from the back of my father's
office. She had already eaten half a dozen and she said to
me:

'You want one, Kit?'

I knew where those snowballs had come from and I was
not attracted. But I also knew that refusal would spoil
what was from Lilli a rare and generous gesture, so I took
one.

'What do they taste like when they're soft?' Lilli asked.

'The same,' I lied, choking down a solid piece of stale
eggwhite.

'Have another,' she said.

But I had done my duty. 'No thanks,' I said. 'I don't like them much anyway.'

I knew that Lilli would eat the remainder rather than take them home to be shared by her brothers and sisters, and I was going on my way when Mrs Small, the owner of the sweet shop, suddenly swooped on Lilli and snatched at the half-eaten box.

'That's absolutely disgusting,' she said. 'You got that box out of the dustbin.'

She tried to take the snowballs away from Lilli, but Lilli's bare feet went quickly to work on Mrs Small's shins and Lilli ran off with the box intact.

'And you, Kit Quayle,' Mrs Small said. 'I'll tell your father what you were doing. It's disgusting.'

I knew better than to argue and I walked off guiltily, feeling some resentment toward Lilli for bringing shame on me, something that Lilli could pay back in kind when she felt like it, but left me helpless in the face of adult threats.

There were incidents like that almost every day in Lilli's life and though her retaliations were usually reserved for the worst insults, she would eventually repay a slight even after six months if the opportunity arose. Mrs Small got her deserts a few weeks later when Lilli locked her in her shop. Mrs Small had a habit of putting her key in the lock outside a few minutes before she emerged to close the shop for the night. Lilli saw the key one night, turned it shut, ran a couple of blocks and threw it over the fence of the local Councillor's house where there was a fierce Alsatian. Nobody had seen Lilli do this but Mrs Small knew who had done it and she surprised Lilli one Saturday morning when she was scavenging the alley. She slapped her hard across the legs, which Lilli accepted as a fair equation under the circumstances, so she ran off without threatening further retaliation.

Lilli's worst retaliation, which involved the police, was on a boy named Poly (Roly-Poly) Howland, the son of the chemist who also bred horses. Poly was four or five years older than Lilli, a big plumpish boy who was spoiled by his mother and who was known among us for his endless, thoughtless teasing which, when directed at smaller children, amounted to bullying. We all detested him, even though we felt sorry for him, and we kept out of his way. But suddenly a cap would be snatched or we would be tripped, pushed, cuffed or mocked for some personal or family defect. Lilli was such an obvious target that week after week she had her hair pulled, or her dress lifted, or she was called 'Gypsy' (a name she hated) or worse for some strange reason: 'Cough-mixture'.

Lilli tried retaliation with feet and nails, but Poly persisted and it looked as if Lilli had finally met her match, although those of us who knew Lilli were sure that she would never give up. It was Friday; we were all leaving school, a special time for one of Poly's pranks, and it came as Lilli expected it to come. She was carrying her sugarbag, which she usually brought to school on Friday ready for her tour of the town's dustbins. Poly snatched it from her and held it high over his head, inviting Lilli to jump if she wanted it back. But Lilli fumbled in some pocket or secret place and produced a penknife which she opened.

'Give me back my sack,' she said to Poly.

Poly looked at the penknife and laughed. 'You're not going to touch me with that,' he said.

'Aren't I,' Lilli said.

In that usual exchange of ultimata that precedes a war Poly said: 'If you do I'll . . .'

He didn't have time to finish his declaration of intent. Lilli sprang on his back, all of her, like a cat, and she plunged the penknife between his shoulder-blades.

I think the only person who wasn't surprised was Lilli. Poly, stunned for a moment, dropped the sack, and Lilli snatched it up and ran off. The blow wasn't very deep and it took a moment for Poly to feel anything. When he did he turned pale and fainted. Someone ran for a teacher and when Poly was picked up his shirt at the back was covered in blood, and for those of us who would record the incident it was memorable that Lilli had not only plunged the knife in, she had pulled it out again and retained it.

The Stubecks were used to police calls. Almost anything stolen in the town meant a visit by Sergeant Collins to the Stubeck house. One of the boys was already in prison for raiding the cigarette kiosk on the railway station. But violence outside the family was not one of their characteristics and Lilli was not only beaten by her father but her mother told one of her older sisters, Grace, to bite her, and I remember those teeth marks on Lilli's arms and legs for weeks afterwards.

It couldn't end there because the whole town soon knew of the incident and not only did parents, concerned for their children, complain to the headmaster of the school, but Mr Howland lodged his complaint with the police so that Lilli had to appear before our local magistrate, Mr E. Badewell, who was also the local Member of the State Legislative Assembly.

Not everyone was willing to condemn Lilli simply because she was a Stubeck. Not everyone liked the Howlands or their children. Two spinsters named Fortune (we called them Luck and Luckless), whom Lilli often begged eggs from, rang my father and asked him if he would attend the magistrate's court to make sure that Lilli's side of the case was heard and that the respectable Howlands didn't have it all their own way.

My father had no sympathy for the Stubecks, even as underdogs, but the legal rights of a citizen, particularly a child, before the law was a simple passion with him, even though he knew that his presence at the magistrate's hearing would be considered a damned silly interference in what was considered an open and shut case. In fact his real problem was not to prove Lilli innocent, because Lilli admitted what she had done and too many children had seen it happen including his own son. All he could hope to do was ameliorate the judicial retribution.

'Did you actually see the incident?' my father asked me.

'We all saw it,' I said.

'I'm not asking about the others, I want to know if you saw it.'

When I said 'Yes' and began to justify Lilli's attack on Poly he stopped me short. 'Tell me what happened,' he insisted, 'not why it happened.'

'That's not fair,' I said. 'It was Poly's fault.'

'Nonetheless, if I have to admit the facts I have to know what they are. So tell me exactly what happened.'

I gave him a blow-by-blow description of the incident and then he said, 'All right. Now tell me why you think she did it.'

It was easy for one of Poly's victims to denounce him, and in the informal hearing before the magistrate my father made attack his best defence. For every accusation against Lilli he replied with a denunciation of Poly's bullying, insisting that some legal restraint be placed on Poly to prevent him provoking such incidents.

In the outcome Lilli was put on probation for a year and Mr Howland was told to discipline his son's behaviour. At no time during the hearing did Matty or Mrs Stubeck show up, which made my father despise them, even though he was secretly pleased that they kept away because their presence would only have prejudiced Lilli's case. He called on Matty Stubeck that night and told him he was very lucky that Lilli hadn't been taken off to Bendigo and put in a state institution. But even that possibility didn't seem to bother Matty or Mrs Stubeck, and my father said contemptuously that it was a waste of time helping the Stubeck family.

'That girl's bound to end up under lock and key one day,' he said and he told my sister and my brother Tom and me to keep away from the whole family. 'They'll always be trouble, so give the lot of them a wide berth.'

There was little likelihood that my sister or Tom or I would ever become involved with the Stubecks, yet I did get involved despite myself. One Saturday morning at six o'clock I crossed the river not far from the Stubecks and began fishing in a favourite backwater. At about eight o'clock I was joined by Lilli who had two lines rolled on corks (stolen, I knew) and a tin of worms. Lilli was a better fisherman than the boys or her father because she was more interested in the river, but by lunchtime she had caught only one perch to my ten.

'How do you do it?' she asked me, walking around to my side of the bend.

'It's luck,' I said.

'Show me what you do,' she insisted.

I showed her how I baited the hooks and where to throw the line, but she said she did all that and still didn't catch anything.

'I told you it's luck,' I said impatiently. 'Anyway I'm going home so you can fish here if you like.'

'No use now,' Lilli said. 'My mother sent me out to see if I could catch some fish for dinner.'

Fishing to me was a sport, but I knew there was no such fancy in Lilli's mind. It was food she wanted, and I foolishly said to her: 'You can have mine if you like.'

'How many have you got?' she asked.

'Ten.'

'That's enough,' she said, and when we were passing her house on The Point she asked me if I wanted to eat some of the fish.

'You mean have dinner at your place?'

'They're your fish,' she said, and I wasn't sure whether I was being included in the Stubeck food collective, whether Lilli was being unusually friendly because of my father's help, or if Lilli finally trusted me enough to take me into that house where nobody went. I remembered my father's warning about the Stubecks, but at the same time I knew a refusal would be taken badly. So I made one modest attempt to avoid it.

'What will your mother say?' I asked her.

'I'll tell her you were going to cook them yourself, and that we're saving you the trouble,' Lilli said.

There was an element of truth in the idea because I would often stay out all Saturday and cook the fish I caught. But what really decided me was an intense desire to know what went on in that unknown household.

'All right,' I said recklessly.

'You stay here,' Lilli told me and, snatching the string of fish from my hand, she went inside. After a moment's silence I heard Mrs Stubeck and Lilli arguing fiercely, then Geordie, one of the older boys, came out and said to me:

'You're a silly bugger, Kit. Do you think you can feed the whole family on ten fish?'

I pointed out that it was Lilli's idea.

'Then she can bloody-well give you her share,' Geordie said.

The meal was an early education for me in the price I would always have to pay for my curiosity. I had to eat a disgusting concoction which I can still remember, and at the end of that meal I would never again look on child-hood and family security in the way that had seemed natural until then.

The Stubeck family, all eleven of them, sat around a big trestle table made of doors in the only room of the house I saw—the smoke-filled kitchen. The walls of the kitchen were smeared with the remnants of food and liquids and graffiti. The uneven table was covered in newspapers which were already stained with food and black rings where saucepans had been set down. The plates were a mixture of tin, enamel and chipped china. I was given a china soup plate which was greasy and cracked. We had spoons and knives but no forks, and there was a fly-covered bottle of tomato sauce on the table which the children were not allowed to touch. I was seated next to Lilli on an old piano stool with the stuffing pulled out of it, and Lilli had taken off her flimsy cotton dress and sat next to me in her cotton drawers which were wet and greasy. Clinging to her shoulder on the other side was little three-fingered Jackie who was now a toddler.

It took me only a few moments to realise that whatever cohesion there was in this family, whatever their collective in scavenging (which I had always respected), there was nothing else between any of them except perhaps between Lilli and little Jackie and maybe the mutual overlordship of Matty and Mrs Stubeck. Otherwise they all behaved like tiger-cubs in a disorderly den. The women—that is the girls and the mother—rarely said anything, but each Stubeck fought for some right of his or her own, not only where to sit but what plate they would have and who could talk and who had to shut up. Slaps, pinches, bites and hearty shoves kept them all occupied, even the adult girls and the older boys. It seemed to be a ritual of physical contact before eating, and Lilli was as fierce with her punches and shoves as the rest, perhaps more so. But it stopped when one of the girls put an enamel basin of cut bread on the table and Mrs Stubeck served the fish.

Mrs Stubeck had boiled my ten perch and Lilli's in a big saucepan of buttermilk. I was given two fish heads in a plate of yellow, fishy milk with an onion in it, and the smell of it was so revolting that I began to breathe through my mouth.

'Put some bread in it,' Lilli said and snatched a piece of bread from the basin and dropped it in my plate. 'Go on. Eat,' she said.

Once again I was the victim of my own commitment, and as I took each mouthful I was sure I couldn't take the next one. Somehow I got through it, and then Mrs Stubeck threw a large boiled onion onto my plate which I hated but which I gulped down hurriedly to get rid of. The meal ended with a cup of tea. Mine came in a china cup without a handle, and though it was marvellously hot it tasted of stale mutton and rancid butter.

It was over tea that the second ritual began, not this time between the children (which the parents had not interfered with) but from Matty who kept order while we drank our tea by leaping up and slapping, pinching or cuffing anyone he could reach. Though there had been yelps of pain and some savage repartee in both rituals, there were no tears and no complaints.

Finally, Matty became very obsequious and begging with me. 'You're a good boy, Kit,' he said.

I kept my eyes on my plate.

'Has your sister got a pair of shoes she can give to Alice?'

'I don't know, Mr Stubeck,' I said.

'Well why don't you look and see if she's got an old pair. She won't miss them.'

'I'll take a look,' I said, and I knew he was asking me to steal them.

'And an old dress for Lilli.'

I looked at Lilli, still holding little Jackie. She was not embarrassed, and when Mrs Stubeck finally roared in her dull voice (the first words she had spoken) that she was not going to fill the teapot again, Lilli pinched my leg and whispered: 'Get out quick.'

I leapt up and was about to say a one-word thankyou to Mrs Stubeck when Lilli pushed me vigorously from behind and told me to hurry up. Outside, she pulled on her dress and said: 'He was going to make you play snap, and you'd have been there all afternoon.'

'Your father plays snap?'

'Yes. Him and the boys, and he always wins,' Lilli said, and I left the Stubeck house that day wondering what it would have been like to play snap with a man like Matty Stubeck and his grown sons. But I was so cured of curiosity about that household that I said goodbye to Lilli at The Point and went home happily to the sanity of my strict hot-tempered father and my gentle pacifist mother. But instead of lying and telling my mother that I had cooked the fish for lunch on the river bank, I foolishly told her that I had given the fish to the Stubecks and said that I had had lunch with them.

'In their house?' my mother said incredulously.

'Yes.'

She said, 'Oh good heavens,' and was thoughtful for a moment. I expected a reprimand, but then she said unhappily, 'That means you'll have to ask Lilli back, Kit.'

That was something that didn't appeal to me at all. 'What for?' I said.

'Common courtesy,' my mother said. 'Particularly with people like that.' My mother meant people who had nothing and gave something, even the Stubecks. But my father was furious when he heard about it and he said to my mother:

'I don't think we have to carry common courtesy that far.'

'Yes, we do,' my mother told him.

He threw up his hands in disgust. 'If you invite them here they'll only come begging,' he said.

Which is exactly what Mrs Stubeck did when eventually, under protest, I invited Lilli for Saturday lunch.

# 3

LILLI AND MRS STUBECK STOOD AT THE BACK DOOR EXPECTING to come in, but my mother guarded the door as Mrs Stubeck said: 'Here she is, Mrs Quayle. It's Lilli.'

'Hello Lilli,' my mother said, calling me to the door.

'Hello Mrs Quayle,' Lilli said. She wore the same dress and no shoes, but for the first time I saw a slide in her untidy black hair.

When it was clear that my mother was keeping the wire door on the latch Mrs Stubeck said: 'Could you let me have a bag of flour, Mrs Quayle, and some potatoes and salt, and anything else you can spare.'

'Well . . . Just a moment,' my mother told her and, leaving Lilli and me looking at each other through the locked wire door, she went into the kitchen and returned eventually with a bundle wrapped in newspaper and a basin of potatoes.

'Give these to Mrs Stubeck,' she said to me, opening the door just enough so that I could put the bundle and the potatoes into Mrs Stubeck's wicker basket. She closed the door behind me.

Leaving no word of public advice to Lilli to be polite, and complaining: 'Is that all you can spare, Mrs Quayle?' Mrs Stubeck left Lilli and me wondering what to do with ourselves until lunch was ready. Lilli settled it by chasing our dog Mickey around the outside of the house. Dogs were known to take to Lilli, and Mickey was no exception, giving her his slave-like attention and begging for her affection. She chased Mickey and then Mickey chased her, and when lunch was called he followed Lilli inside and sat under the table licking her dusty bare feet.

For a moment I wondered if Lilli was going to take off her dress, but she sat still and watched my father as if only he could dictate the terms of our behaviour. When he closed his eyes and said grace Lilli was fascinated. When he carved the Saturday joint of beef and gave her the first helping (with vegetables) she attacked it without waiting for the rest of us to be served.

I nudged her. 'You have to wait,' I whispered.

'What for?'

'Until he's finished.'

'Oh.'

She put down the knife and fork and watched the rest of the table like a tiger-cub waiting to pounce. My sister and my brother Tom were as fascinated with Lilli as she was with them, but when she caught Tom staring at her she grimaced at him and made one of her silent hissing miaows. Then she asked me in a whisper if she could have some tomato sauce.

'Can Lilli have some tomato sauce?' I asked my mother.

'You know very well we don't have any tomato sauce, Kit,' my mother said. My father would allow Worcestershire Sauce in the house but not tomato sauce which he considered an Australian vulgarity. 'We haven't got any, Lilli, and I don't think you need it.'

We all watched her using fork, knife and spoon to collect her food, and she was first to finish, eating noisily and with urgent preoccupation.

'Is that all? Can we go now?' she whispered to me when she had finished.

'There's going to be angel cake.' I said.

'What's that?'

'It's pudding, it's sweet,' I said.

'Kit,' my father said. 'Whatever you and Lilli want to say to each other you can say it loud enough for the rest of us to hear.'

'She was only asking me if there was anything else.'

'It won't be long, Lilli,' my mother said, and when she gave Lilli the first helping of pudding Lilli waited for everyone else to be served. But once again it was a noisy plunging attack that demolished the pudding long before

Tom had finished, and Tom was usually the first to finish. Lilli's fingers had been thoroughly immersed in the business of eating, and ignoring the clean napkin my mother had laid on the table near her she lifted her dress and wiped them on her drawers. Then, realising that Mickey was still under foot, she gave him her hand to lick clean, nudging me happily when Micky had finished.

'Now?' she said with that Stubeck instinct to get out before Matty could do any harm.

'You have to wait,' I said.

She fidgeted restlessly and tousled Mickey's head and nudged me impatiently until my father put his napkin in its ivory ring and we did likewise.

'Now,' I said.

Lilli exploded from her chair saying 'Come on Mickey' and was out of the dining room and through the back door before my father had pushed back his chair.

It was only when my sister cleared the table and put the napkins away that she discovered the loss of Lilli's unused napkin. Lilli had quietly tucked it into her drawers, and though my mother sighed for the loss of one of her good damask dinner napkins she didn't tell my father and she did not tell me to try to get it back. But she did say that night over supper: 'I'm sorry for that girl, with no one to teach her what is right and what is wrong.'

In fact Lilli was about to find herself with someone who would try to teach her right from wrong and in the process create for her another kind of life which she would both accept and resist in her fierce determination to remain the only person she wanted to be, which was Lilli Stubeck.

# 4

MISS DALGLEISH WAS, I SUPPOSE, AN ANOMALY IN OUR TOWN, although it is impossible to think of St Helen without her curious, mincing figure and the big old house she lived in behind its high wooden wall. Old Mr Dalgleish, her father, whom I can just remember, was one of the wheat and wool Dalgleishes, a family whose name was connected in London as well as Australia with the old colonial trade in wheat, wool, hides, skins, fertilisers and anything else that made money out of Australian farming.

His branch of the family were no longer connected with the business but he was wealthy enough nonetheless to live at his leisure in Europe for long periods. In fact we always wondered why he and his daughter (who was in her early sixties when her father was in his late eighties) returned to our town. I remember him as a stiff, upright old man with a large cyst on the back of his neck aggravated by the high starched collars he wore. Though his money came from wool and wheat, and though our town was at the very heart of the wool and wheat district of Victoria, he had nothing to do with any of it. He was strictly a money man, and twice a week he would walk slow and upright to one of the banks, which he had some interest in, and spend the morning in an office going over his affairs. The rest of the time he would disappear behind the high wooden wall of his house in the main street and only emerge from time to time to go to church or visit the Eyres—the other wealthy family who ran the Riverain station across the river—hiring one of Mr Malone's Marmons or Chevrolets to take him there and bring him back.

Miss Dalgleish was in Europe when her father died, but

relatives came up from Melbourne, and the old man was given a big funeral which every important citizen in the town (including my father) attended.

'What do you think she'll do when she comes back?' my mother asked my father when they began speculating on Miss Dalgleish's future.

'The old man was well over eighty and she's in her sixties, so I can't imagine her making any drastic move.'

'But what'll she do in that big house all alone?'

'There's always Mrs Stone.'

When we thought of the Dalgleishes we also thought of Mrs Stone who had lived with them for more than thirty years. She had once been some kind of maid-companion to Miss Dalgleish and had been to Europe several times with father and daughter. But we knew her as the one person in the town who came and went freely to and from that house. She was a pleasant, homely, intelligent woman who was in her seventies when Mr Dalgleish died, but still very active and healthy. Her husband, Jeff Stone, had been some sort of gardener-stableman when the Dalgleishes had kept a horse and buggy, but when Mr Stone was killed in the First World War Mr Dalgleish had sold them and never bothered thereafter with anything but hired transport and a twice-weekly gardener called Bob Andrews who was deaf and dumb.

Mrs Stone had been given the official status of 'house-keeper' by the town, although an old scandal suggested that she had also become Mr Dalgleish's mistress. It might have been true, but she was such a friendly and unaffected woman, with such bright blue eyes and vigorous grey hair that most people either ignored the rumour or simply didn't care whether it was true or not. To that extent the Dalgleishes were above any serious condemnation for mis-behaviour; to that extent too they made their own rules for behaviour. Particularly Miss Dalgleish.

What we knew of Miss Dalgleish was part hearsay, part fact and more than half speculation. She always dressed in long soft Edwardian gowns (silk tussore in summer) with pointed shoes that had waisted heels. She almost always wore a long string of jet beads and carried a soft leather handbag with a tortoiseshell handle, and though we often tried to guess what was in that handbag it was only when I asked Lilli much later that I discovered it was books: a novel in French or German or Italian, and with it the appropriate pocket dictionary.

It was her connection with European culture that really set her apart from the rest of us, even more than her money, because that high wooden wall not only gave the Dalgleishes their personal privacy, it became a cultural frontier separating us from what went on behind it. We knew she had a large library of books in several languages, curious modern paintings, naked sculpture, other large objects and an unusual library of foreign opera records, some of which came to Miss Dalgleish from abroad. Most of her books and records came through the mail from Melbourne, as if our local book and record shops were hardly up to her needs, although they were both excellent. But she did patronise them sometimes, as if she had to do her local duty by them.

What almost everyone in the town found flattering was a greeting from Miss Dalgleish. Her father had never greeted anyone himself, although he would always reply to a greeting with grave courtesy, even from children. Miss Dalgleish on the other hand would, in her rather prim voice, say good morning or good afternoon or good evening, but never good night to those she chose to recognise. ('Good night,' she would say, 'is a termination,' and she hated terminations.) And if she added your name to a greeting it became an accolade.

I can still remember the pride I felt when she first said to me 'Good morning, Kit,' as I passed her one Saturday morning, walking upright like her father along our main street.

'Good morning, Miss Dalgleish,' I replied.

She stopped me that day with a little tap on the shoulder and, startled, I turned around to face her.

'You should part your hair on the other side,' she told me. 'Then it would not stand up in rebellion as it does now.'

I was so flattered that when I went home I wet my hair

and shifted the parting to the other side (the 'girl's side')
and have kept it that way ever since.

When Miss Dalgleish came home from Europe after her
father's death the town began speculating on two problems:
how much money had she inherited, and how long would
she stay in St Helen this time. The amount of money she
inherited remained a Dalgleish secret, but six months
later there was no sign of Miss Dalgleish leaving, and it
looked as if her father's death had given her some reason
for staying on, though we didn't know what the reason
was. Certainly Mrs Stone would never tell us because she
refused to talk of what went on in that house. Yet it was
odd how Miss Dalgleish for her part knew everything that
was happening in the town.

'Why do you defend a man who beats his wife?' Miss
Dalgleish asked my father the day he appeared in court
defending a man called Jock MacLeish.

'Because he's not in court for beating his wife,' my
father told her, surprised that she knew about it.

'Does it matter?' she said. 'He's a frightful man.'

'His character has nothing to do with it, Miss Dalgleish.
He's being sued for non-payment of a debt, and he has a
right to a proper defence.'

'Such men should never be defended on any account,'
Miss Dalgleish insisted, and though my father hated
anyone telling him what the rights of man were or were
not, he accepted it from Miss Dalgleish because she was a
cultured woman.

The routine of the Dalgleish house remained much the
same except that we no longer saw the old man on his way
to the bank or the church. Miss Dalgleish now wore black
but otherwise she didn't change her habits or her manner.
Mrs Stone still did the shopping, cooking and cleaning,
and it looked as if Miss Dalgleish and Mrs Stone had
settled down to a quiet existence which would last for
many years.

But about a year after the old man's death Mrs Stone
became ill. Some said it was kidneys, others rheumatoid
arthritis, but overnight she was frequently bedridden and
Miss Dalgleish had to find someone to look after Mrs

Stone and the house. Much as she disliked the idea it had to be a local woman, and finally a Mrs Peters was employed to come in at 9 o'clock every morning to attend to the house and to Mrs Stone, cook lunch, prepare a cold supper and leave at 4 o'clock. That was all Mrs Peters could manage because she had a family of two grown sons and a husband who worked as a mechanic at Malone's garage. Mrs Peter's real advantages were her cleanliness and taciturnity. She was thin-bodied and thin-lipped and she had a reputation for minding her own business to the point of rudeness. In any case it seemed no more than a temporary arrangement.

What brought Lilli and Miss Dalgleish together was another emergency. Mrs Stone's health had not improved and Miss Dalgleish was reluctant to leave her bedside. It was Thursday afternoon and a pain-killer was urgently needed from the chemist. Unfortunately Howland's delivery boy was out and, as Mrs Peters had already left for the day, Miss Dalgleish opened the big wooden gate and watched for the first passing boy or girl who could be commissioned to go to the chemist. Lilli was the first to pass, and though Miss Dalgleish knew very well who she was and her reputation in the town she nonetheless offered Lilli a shilling if she would run the errand.

'And another shilling if you are quick,' Miss Dalgleish said.

Lilli was eleven. She now wore shoes—battered and broken, but shoes nonetheless. She took them off, tucked them under her arm with the empty medicine bottle and was off down the street before Miss Dalgleish had closed and locked the big wooden gate behind her.

When that big gate was locked it could only be opened without a key from inside, and though there was a bellpull to the house Lilli ignored it on her return. She had been into this garden by her own route before, and she simply climbed the high wooden wall by using the neighbour's fence as a stepping stone and dropping down into the vegetable garden.

'How did you get in?' Miss Dalgleish asked when Lilli appeared at the front door.

'Over the fence,' Lilli said.

'I don't like that at all,' Miss Dalgleish told her. 'But you were very quick so here's your two shillings.'

Two shillings to Lilli was a bonanza, and with an eye to the future she asked Miss Dalgleish if she wanted anything else in the town.

'I don't want anything in town,' Miss Dalgleish replied. 'But come back tomorrow after your school and I might have something else for you to do.'

'All right,' Lilli said.

'But ring the bell. Don't ever climb the fence.'

'Can I take a pomegranate?'

There were four pomegranate bushes along one side of the Dalgleish garden and they were laden with fruit.

'You can take one, but be sure you don't break the bushes or step on the flowerbeds.'

Lilli didn't have her sugarbag with her but she filled her skirt and I passed her on the way home biting into the split bitter skin of a pomegranate with her strong white teeth and sucking out the seeds. She told me what had happened, and I asked her what was behind that high wooden wall, what was inside the house.

'What do you want to know for?' she said.

'Everybody wants to know,' I told her. I wanted to know about the 'naked' statues.

'Well they're not going to find out from me,' Lilli said and I wasn't sure whether she was loyally guarding the Dalgleish secrets, or whether she was simply refusing to contribute anything to the town's curiosity (although plenty of tradesmen supplying the Dalgleishes knew what was behind that wall).

Lilli went back to the house the next day and Miss Dalgleish asked her to push Mrs Stone around the large garden in a wheelchair which had just been delivered from Melbourne. Lilli spent an hour with Mrs Stone and thereafter she returned every day after school to do the same thing. A few weeks later Lilli began to run other errands for Miss Dalgleish—to the post office, to the bank (with letters not money) and to the shops when Mrs Peters was too busy to go. The only time I saw Lilli with anything that might have been stolen from Miss Dalgleish was one Friday evening when I saw her hurrying home with a full sugarbag and two peacock feathers which were too large and delicate to be put in her bag.

'Where did you get them?' I asked her.

'Found them,' she said.

'What do you think you'll do with them?'

'That's my business,' she said.

In fact she gave one of them to Dorothy Malone who still shared a desk with her, and though Dorothy didn't know where that feather came from she knew very well that anything Lilli gave her was acquired in the Stubeck way.

As Mrs Stone's condition worsened, Miss Dalgleish used Lilli more and more for small items of help inside as well as outside the house. Finally a full-time nurse from one of the private hospitals was brought in, and Lilli became aide-de-camp for the trio of women who were there to make sure that Mrs Stone, in her agony, lacked for nothing.

One Saturday morning at 4 a.m. Mrs Stone died, and when she was buried on the Wednesday, Miss Dalgleish buried her alone, walking stiffly behind the cortege and turning away the moment the Presbyterian Minister, Mr Armitage, had finished the ceremony. Mrs Stone's death was nothing to do with anyone but herself and she made her way back to the car without saying a word to anyone, not even to the Reverend Armitage.

From the day that Lilli had begun to run messages for Miss Dalgleish the town had been very curious about her attendance on the old lady, wondering how on earth Miss Dalgleish could have chosen a Stubeck to help her. But what now? The speculation in our house was the same as it was in almost every other house in town.

'Miss Dalgleish will have to get someone else to replace Mrs Stone,' my mother said. 'She's not likely to depend on Mrs Peters and Lilli Stubeck to run that house.'

'There's nothing much to run it for,' my father pointed out. 'Just Miss Dalgleish herself.'

'Nonetheless the old lady is very particular.'

Once again we all expected some sort of change in Miss Dalgleish's behaviour that would reflect her new situation; after all she was now quite alone. But once again Miss Dalgleish went on behaving in exactly the same way, apparently content to allow Mrs Peters and Lilli to satisfy her needs. In fact it became routine to see Lilli coming and going from the Dalgleish house after school or during the day in the summer holidays. The curious thing is that nobody knew how they behaved towards each other or what was said between them, or even what Lilli did for Miss Dalgleish (apart from running messages). Mrs Peters remained her thin, silent self, so the mystery continued until one day the Stubecks disappeared.

It was my brother Tom who came home from swimming in the hole near The Point and reported that they had decamped.

'The house is empty and the horse and cart and everything else have gone. The whole lot of them,' he said.

It didn't really surprise anyone because the Stubecks had always been considered itinerants who would one day disappear the way they had come. Their old cart was seen by someone fully laden on the way to Bendigo, the nearest big town. Later it was reported somewhere else, and finally it was lost sight of because nobody was interested any more.

What surprised us ('Amazing!' my father said) was the extraordinary discovery that Lilli Stubeck had been left behind with Miss Dalgleish.

# 5

LILLI WAS VIRTUALLY BOUGHT AND PAID FOR BY MISS DAL-gleish. She gave Matty Stubeck thirty pounds for Lilli; it may not have been as crude a transaction as a simple statement like that suggests, but the money did change hands even though it was not what Miss Dalgleish originally intended. It simply happened when Lilli told Miss Dalgleish the day before the family decamped that she would not be coming back any more because they were all leaving St Helen for good the next day.

I know what happened that day because Lilli eventually gave me a primitive account of it in a black book which she kept and which needs a little more explanation later on. And though Lilli didn't write it this way, I know that what follows is a fairly accurate account of what was said.

Miss Dalgleish asked Lilli where the family was going to.

'I don't know,' Lilli said.

It was not a situation that Miss Dalgleish, being a Dalgleish, was going to accept.

'Are they taking you far away?' Miss Dalgleish asked her.

'How do I know?' Lilli said.

'Doesn't your father tell you anything?'

'He wouldn't tell us a thing like that,' Lilli replied scornfully.

'Then perhaps he'll tell me,' Miss Dalgleish said. 'Tell your father to come and see me tonight, Lilli. I want to know where you're going and what he intends to do with you.'

'What do you want to know that for?' Lilli demanded.

'Never mind. Just tell him I insist on seeing him.'

'Here?'

'Yes. And your mother too.'

'They'll only ask you for food or something,' Lilli pointed out.

'That's not the point.'

'You'll tell them that I said we were going away.'

'Well?'

'That means I'll get bitten . . .'

'Bitten? Don't be silly. If you don't tell them to come and see me I'll ring Mr Malone and he can take me down to your place.'

'All right. I'll tell him,' Lilli said, and that night Matty and Mrs Stubeck, with Lilli behind them, were admitted to the kitchen of the Dalgleish fortress to explain themselves to Miss Dalgleish.

It was a curious interview because the Stubecks didn't know what Miss Dalgleish wanted of them, and it was only during the discussion that Miss Dalgleish herself seemed to decide what she wanted. At first it was all cross purpose. The Stubecks were begging flour, sugar, money and old clothes, but Miss Dalgleish was trying to find out where they were going and for how long. Neither side would give way, either to the begging or to any questions about destinations.

Finally Miss Dalgleish said, 'All right, Mr Stubeck. You can go where you like but I think it would be best if you left Lilli with me.'

'What for?' Matty asked her.

'Because I need her.'

'What for?' Matty said again.

'I told you. I need her here. I'll see that she attends school and is properly dressed and behaves herself.'

'You mean she'll live here with you?' Mrs Stubeck said.

'Of course that's what I mean. There's a room upstairs for her.' (It was one of the few houses in town that had two storeys.) 'And she can stay here with me until you come back.'

'But what do you want her for, Miss?' Matty persisted. 'What's the matter with telling me what you want her for?'

'Nothing is the matter. She can do small things for me.

Being present when I need her. She can help Mrs Peters on Saturday and with the breakfasts. I want her here, that's all.'

So far Lilli herself had not been consulted, and neither side seemed to consider it important, even as Matty Stubeck now began bargaining.

'We need Lilli ourselves, Miss Dalgleish,' he said. 'She's a lot quicker than the others.' Matty meant that she was a better scavenger and pilferer than the rest of the family, and Miss Dalgleish understood perfectly what was meant.

'She won't need to do anything like that here,' she said firmly.

'What about us?' Mrs Stubeck said. 'She's worth a lot to us, Miss.'

Miss Dalgleish knew now what was involved and she told Lilli to go outside in the hall and wait there.

'What for?' Lilli said, refusing to move.

'Do as you're told,' Matty said, raising his hand.

Lilli went into the hall and Miss Dalgleish said: 'How much is she worth to you Mrs Stubeck?'

'She's a good girl,' Matty said.

'I know that. But if being a good girl is what she's worth to you, then you can see the advantages she'll have here. She can earn a little money and send it on to you.'

'How much?'

'Never mind how much. I'll give her what she deserves and I'll make sure you get some of it.'

Matty now began to point out that they might be travelling; it was difficult to send money through the post; someone might steal it. And anyway he would have to know how much. In fact if Miss Dalgleish would give him some money now . . .

Matty left the sentence unfinished and Miss Dalgleish said again: 'How much, Mr Stubeck?'

'Fifty pounds now is all I ask. Then she wouldn't have to send us anything more. Fifty pounds would be fair, Miss Dalgleish. She's a good girl and she's clean, the cleanest one in the family.'

'You mean you'll leave her with me if I give you fifty pounds? Is that what you're saying?'

'If you want her that's what's fair, Miss Dalgleish.'

'What do you say, Mrs Stubeck?'

'She's my daughter, Missus, so it's the least we can do if you'll look after her.'

'I'll give you twenty-five pounds and not a penny more,' Miss Dalgleish said, 'And even so it's quite shameful.'

'Are you going to send us money afterwards?' Matty asked.

'No. I said that was all I would give you.'

'It's not enough, Miss Dalgleish,' Matty complained. 'She'll be working properly soon, and she looks after our Jackie.'

'I'll give you thirty pounds, Mr Stubeck, but on the firm condition that you leave Lilli entirely to me without any attachments.'

Matty wanted to know what that meant—'without any attachments'.

'It means that if you come back and ask for more money later on,' Miss Dalgleish said, 'I'll simply send Lilli back to you.'

'How do you know she'll want to stay with you?' Matty said.

'You must ask her yourself,' Miss Dalgleish replied and called Lilli in from the hall where she had been listening at the door to everything said.

Lilli came in very slowly and stood between Matty and Miss Dalgleish looking from one to the other with her cat-like eyes.

Matty gave her a rough little push as if to warn her that he was not going to take any nonsense from her and he said aggressively, 'Do you want to stay here with Miss Dalgleish, Lilli? You want to stay here in this big house and help the old lady?'

Lilli went on looking from one to the other without saying anything.

'Well?' Matty said, giving her another little push.

'What does *she* say?' Lilli said, pointing to her mother.

'You'd better be a good girl and don't answer back,' Mrs Stubeck said threateningly.

'How long do you want me to stay?' Lilli asked calmly.

'Never mind how long for,' Matty said. 'Just do as you're told, pumpkin.'

Lilli knew she had an advantage on both sides and she wasn't going to let it go. 'Will I be your daughter now?' she asked Miss Dalgleish.

'No, you will not,' Miss Dalgleish said firmly. 'But I'll treat you as well as I would treat anyone in my own family, Lilli.'

'If I'm not going to be your daughter why do you want me to stay?' Lilli asked her.

'You can only have one mother,' Miss Dalgleish said, 'and I don't wish to take her place. But if you stay here you can help me and Mrs Peters around the house and I'll help you with your school work and see that you are properly dressed and looked after.'

'But you won't let me do anything, will you,' Lilli said.

Matty cuffed her and Lilly rubbed her ear but persisted. 'Can I swim when I want to?' she said to Miss Dalgleish.

'That will depend on the circumstances,' Miss Dalgleish said cautiously. 'But if you're going to be afraid of me or suspicious of me, Lilli, then you'd better not stay.'

'I'm not afraid of you,' Lilli said boldly.

'You're too damned cheeky,' Matty said and cuffed her again.

'Oh, enough of that,' Miss Dalgleish said to Matty. 'I won't hit you Lilli, but you'll have to do as you're told. And I'm not promising you anything more than I want to promise you. Do you understand?'

'Yes,' Lilli said.

'Well?' Miss Dalgleish said to Matty.

'All right,' Matty said. 'She can stay if she wants to.'

'And you, Lilli?'

'I don't mind,' Lilli said magnanimously, and before Matty could demand his money in front of Lilli Miss Dalgleish told him to come back the next morning after 11 o'clock and they would settle everything.

'But don't you tell anyone we're leaving,' Matty said to Miss Dalgleish. 'I don't want busybodies trying to stop us.'

'Who would want to stop you, Mr Stubeck? In any case what you do is your own affair,' Miss Dalgleish said. 'It's nothing to do with me.'

'Do you want Lilli to stay here tonight?' Mrs Stubeck said.

'If she wants to.'

'Can you let me have some flour and sugar,' Mrs Stubeck begged. 'And some potatoes and soap?'

'Oh, very well,' Miss Dalgleish said. 'Lilli. You know where everything is. Give your mother what she wants, and if you want to stay here tonight you can do so.'

She left the kitchen to the Stubecks, which no one else in the town would have done, and somewhere in that old wicker basket Mrs Stubeck had enough empty tins and containers for Lilli to fill with flour, sugar, salt, pepper, potatoes, tea, biscuits, treacle and bread. Then she said, 'Goodbye, Mum,' as Mrs Stubeck looked hungrily around the well-stocked kitchen.

'Goodbye Lill,' Mrs Stubeck said, and taking a bright yellow brooch she always wore on her bosom she placed it on Lilli's dress and said, 'It's my best, so look after it.'

And, seeing them out, Lilli slammed the big gate behind them with the kind of authority that comes with a new possession. In fact Lilli would not see any of the Stubecks again until the day that two of them came into town to claim her back.

# 6

NOBODY QUITE BELIEVED IT AT FIRST, EXPECTING LILLI TO BE collected next day or put on a train or delivered somewhere in the family wake. What convinced us that Lilli was actually going to stay indefinitely was the sight of Miss Dalgleish and Lilli walking down the street to Williams the draper's shop. Inside that dry old store, the biggest in town, Miss Dalgleish asked for Mr Williams himself, and he stepped down from his office which was set rather high in the shop where little cylinders with bills or money in them were sent up to him on taut piano wires.

'Good morning, Mr Williams,' Miss Dalgleish said.

'Good morning, Miss Dalgleish,' Mr Williams replied, eyeing Lilli curiously. 'Hello, Lilli,' he said. He was a popular, friendly man whose son had once lost a bicycle to the thieving Stubeck boys but he wasn't the sort to take it out on Lilli.

Lilli said nothing; she seemed to be there reluctantly and she had a way of removing herself.

'I want some clothes for Lilli,' Miss Dalgleish said to Mr Williams, 'but I don't know what size she is. So if you will give me a young woman who knows about children's clothes I'll give her the list of what I want.'

'Let me see the list,' Mr Williams said.

'I prefer to deal with one of your young ladies,' Miss Dalgleish told him.

'All right, Miss Dalgleish, but we may not have everything you want. We're waiting for a delivery of girls' outfitting next week.'

'If you haven't got what we need we'll come back Mr Williams.'

Mr Williams said: 'Joanie, come over here will you,' and they were joined by Joan Collingwood, the daughter of our local postman. Mr Williams told her to look after Miss Dalgleish, and with a conspiratorial wink at Lilli as if they both knew she was on to a good thing, Mr Williams returned to his office.

That list of clothing was the final proof we needed of Miss Dalgleish's commitment to Lilli. Not only did the list ask for dresses, jumpers, aprons, underwear, nightgowns, shoes and stockings, it also wanted two complete school uniforms of navy blue blazers, tunics and white blouses, because Lilli would be in her first year at our new High School when the school year began in a few weeks' time.

Lilli didn't say a word to Miss Dalgleish or to Joan Collingwood while she was being outfitted. She was neither sullen nor subdued, just still, and it was Miss Dalgleish who decided if the shoes and clothes were too big or too small, and what colour the cotton dresses should be.

'Send it all around tomorrow before eleven,' Miss Dalgleish said when Mr Williams descended again from his office and glanced at the pile of clothing on one of the counters.

'Did we have everything you need, Miss Dalgleish?'

'More or less,' she replied, and after thanking Mr Williams and Joan she said, 'Come on, Lilli,' and they left the shop and walked back to the house, closing that big wooden gate behind them on this new aspect of Dalgleish behaviour; there was obviously not going to be any public or even private explanation of Lilli's presence.

It may seem extraordinary today but it was perfectly normal then for the town to accept Lilli as the ward of Miss Dalgleish. I suppose most people felt that Lilli would be far better off with Miss Dalgleish than she was with her own thieving family, and nobody doubted that Miss Dalgleish's motives were honest and aboveboard, however strange it all seemed.

Nonetheless there were plenty of unanswered questions that intrigued us. What arrangement had Miss Dalgleish made with Matty Stubeck and his wife about Lilli? Was Lilli there as some sort of servant? Was she a new sort of companion-maid? In fact, what was Miss Dalgleish's true motive? What was her real reason for keeping Lilli? When Lilli's time among us eventually ran out I would be the only person who would know some of the answers to these questions, and the information would come from Lilli's black book. I don't want to be ahead of myself in explaining how I got it, but even the reason for Lilli's black book is significant.

Lilli discovered in those first few weeks with Miss Dalgleish that she was keeping an account of everything Lilli did. Inevitably, it also became an account of what Miss Dalgleish thought and felt about Lilli, and no day passed without Miss Dalgleish adding to it. When she realised that Lilli had found it and was reading it, Miss Dalgleish thereafter kept it locked in a desk drawer, and it was in retaliation for that little book of Miss Dalgleish's that Lilli began to keep one of her own. She used a school exercise book and, though the early entries are childish, later on they become better though rather spasmodic. In fact there is just enough information in Lilli's book to fill in many of the gaps which otherwise would have remained a mystery.

But this would come to me much later. Now it was enough to know that Lilli was definitely going to stay with Miss Dalgleish, and if anybody was seriously troubled by the situation Miss Dalgleish certainly was not, nor was Lilli. They were now in each other's domain, and the course of Lilli's 'tragedy' had been set.

# 7

PERHAPS NOTHING OF WHAT FOLLOWS WILL BE UNDERSTOOD unless I say something about their different motives, and again I am taking Lilli's word for it because I think she eventually became a fair judge of why Miss Dalgleish wanted her, and what she, as an eleven year old, wanted in return.

What Lilli didn't know was how long she would stay with Miss Dalgleish. She thought of it at first as nothing more than a temporary lapse from family responsibilities. Someday she would go back. In the meantime there was too much that was tempting in this extraordinary, old and rich house for Lilli to think of refusing. Miss Dalgleish on the other hand had a far more complicated plan for Lilli. She had already found something in Lilli that she wanted. Lilli was not only a silent messenger and the guardian-of-herself-in-waiting, but she was a ready-made Galatea whom Miss Dalgleish could reconstruct to become a faithful attendant in her old age; a youthful one, too, who would be there when she was needed, who would be vigorous to the end, and lasting, not like Mrs Stone who had died too soon to do her final duty for Miss Dalgleish.

And there was something else.

Even as a child Lilli didn't ask anybody to be sentimental with her and didn't expect it. Miss Dalgleish liked this aspect of Lilli's half-formed personality and knew it was ideal for what she wanted. She hated sentimentality herself. This meant that from the outset they were both incapable of showing any deeper sentiment towards each other than the mere regulation of how they got on together, which left them living outside each other as permanent strangers, even when they were forced to come to terms on the simplest things, such as behaviour, dress, manners and school work. There was no way that any warmth could come into it, so their first steps at adaption were almost impersonal on both sides.

In fact both began the relationship determined not to reshape themselves in any way. Whatever plans Miss Dalgleish had for her, Lilli was determined to remain Lilli, and I think that this aspect of their relationship more than anything else decided almost everything that would happen to them, because it created a curious contest between them which would eventually harden into a matter of survival for Lilli. It also hid the other side of Lilli Stubeck which Miss Dalgleish never reached, and which Lilli would never give up, and this side of Lilli's personality played its part in almost everything she did.

The first night Lilli spent in the house Miss Dalgleish helped her make up the bed in the small room upstairs, gave her a cotton blouse which would serve as a nightgown and told her to wash her face and feet before she got into bed. Lilli thought the whole idea silly, but she liked water and never minded soaking herself in it. She obliged with her feet. What she objected to was the blouse, because she had always slept naked except for her knickers. When Miss Dalgleish told her to take them off and wear the blouse Lilli said 'Not on your life'. Despite her reckless lack of prudery Lilli said that sleeping without her knickers on was dangerous, even though she didn't care whether she had them on or not during the daytime. She refused to wear a nightgown even when Miss Dalgleish bought one for her, and though they would continue to argue about it Lilli never gave way and always slept naked except for her knickers.

What Lilli did have to allow for was Miss Dalgleish's interest in how she looked and behaved, because Lilli had never had to contend with care or criticism of her appearance from her own family. It was a double-edged problem for her: on the one hand the novel feeling that someone was actually concerned, and on the other hand the fact that Miss Dalgleish was telling her what she should wear and even how she should wear it. The nightgown was only one aspect. Lilli had to face an even more complicated situation when Miss Dalgleish came up to her room on the first morning of school and watched her getting dressed in her new school uniform.

Looking her over from head to toe, straightening her tie, tightening her belt (around the hips in those days) and then tugging and pulling her into shape, Miss Dalgleish was not quite satisfied and she realised what was wrong. She sent Mrs Peters to her own bedroom for a hairbrush and some hairclips and, telling Lilli to stand still, she brushed Lilli's curly, black, gypsy-ish hair into some sort of discipline, finally pinning it back behind her ears.

Lilli had no memory of anyone dressing her before; she had no recollection at all of her mother even pulling a dress over her head. The experience was so unique that she relaxed into it with a sort of amazed sensual pleasure, and when Miss Dalgleish held her hair and brushed it out and fiddled with it, Lilli had stared at herself in the mirror as if she were watching a toy being played with, a strange doll in someone else's hands.

'You must brush it morning and evening every day, Lilli,' Miss Dalgleish told her.

'What for?' Lilli said.

Miss Dalgleish didn't say that she had to keep it clean and tidy. She said: 'Because you are growing up and you must learn to look after yourself and your appearance.'

Lilli said nothing, but when she was outside and on the way to school she mussed up her hair because she knew that it would be noticed. Then she stopped halfway to school and took off the new black bloomers which had elastic around the legs. She hid them in Mrs Royce's thick hedge and went on to school, preferring nothing at all to the imprisonment of those black, bloomered drawers. We all noticed Lilli's new clothes, and it was so incongruous to see Lilli looking neat and tidy that only the old threat of fierce retaliation stopped us saying anything — all except Dorothy Malone who said: 'You look marvellous, Lill!'

Inevitably her bare backside was seen by half the school and by one of the teachers, and Lilli was sent for by Miss

Hazel, the head woman teacher, who knew all about Lilli and knew too that she would have to handle her carefully for the sake of Miss Dalgleish.

'Where are your bloomers, Lilli?' Miss Hazel said.

'I lost them,' Lilli replied.

'That's not an answer. Where did you put them?'

'In Mrs Royce's hedge,' Lilli said, unable to bother with a lie for very long.

'Then you had better go and get them, Miss Hazel told her. 'You can't come to school without bloomers on.'

'I don't like them.'

'Nonetheless you have to wear them. Go and get them.'

'Now?'

'Yes, now. And if I see you without them again I'll have to telephone Miss Dalgleish and tell her.'

'She wouldn't care.'

'Oh, yes she would. Now go and put them on.'

Lilli collected the bloomers but as she stood in the middle of the footpath and pulled them on she was seen by old Mrs Royce who owned our local newspaper, and it was Mrs Royce who thought it very funny and told Miss Dalgleish. When Miss Dalgleish questioned Lilli and discovered that she hated the elasticised legs and refused to wear them, she tried to insist.

'Every girl in the school wears them,' Miss Dalgleish pointed out.

'Not me,' Lilli said firmly. 'I'll take them off and wear my old ones. I'm not going to wear them.'

'You must.'

'No!' Lilli said.

'I shall punish you, Lilli.'

Lilli waited for a pinch, a bite, a blow—though she knew none was likely. 'How?' she said to Miss Dalgleish.

'I shan't let you go swimming.'

Lilli knew that nobody was going to stop her swimming. 'I'm going to wear my own knickers,' she said.

In fact Miss Dalgleish compromised and took Lilli back to Williams the draper's and bought her some black knickers which Lilli wore thereafter. Moreover this established a fashion among the other girls that they too should be allowed to wear knickers instead of bloomers, even though it meant that their black stockings were inclined to fall down without that extra help in keeping them up.

I suppose it was part adaptation, part the beginning of their complex relationship, but Lilli and Miss Dalgleish soon found out that there were certain things that they both had to accept as settled although they were by no means settled. Lilli was given a key to the gate and told never to climb the walls, back or front. But Lilli still came and went over the wooden wall when she felt like it until Miss Dalgleish said that every time she did so meant the loss of a 'dessert' as supper. Since Lilli was not used to a 'dessert' anyway it was no punishment to do without it, so this left them cancelling each other out.

The routine of the house was so well established that Lilli had to fit into it, even though she would still come and go as she pleased. Lilli was such an early riser that she didn't mind doing her duty by lighting the wood fire in the kitchen for Mrs Peters in the morning. She was used to doing it at The Point. She was fascinated by the little electric stove (one of the first in the town) and the electric kettle, and she would fry her own eggs on the electric stove and make her tea with the electric kettle before Mrs Peters arrived for the day, or before Miss Dalgleish came downstairs for her own breakfast. She washed her own dishes by running them briefly under the cold water tap, until Mrs Peters told her to leave them so that they could be washed up properly.

'No,' Miss Dalgleish insisted. 'Show her how to do it properly Mrs Peters and let her wash them herself.'

'She'll break them,' Mrs Peters said.

'I don't think so,' Miss Dalgleish said.

It was said in front of Lilli, and in all the time she was with Miss Dalgleish Lilli never did break a plate in the act of washing it.

What Miss Dalgleish found repulsive were Lilli's table manners, or rather the way she contorted her face when eating or when she cleaned her teeth afterwards with her tongue.

'Go upstairs and get me the big mirror on my dressing

table,' Miss Dalgleish told Lilli as they sat down to eat their supper together after a week of it.

When Lilli returned with the mirror Miss Dalgleish propped it up in front of Lilli and said: 'Now look at yourself when you eat and see how awful you look when you contort your face that way.'

'What difference does it make?' Lilli protested.

'It makes a difference to me because I have to watch you,' Miss Dalgleish said. 'Good table manners are not for your benefit but for the benefit of others.'

Lilli had to go on eating before the mirror until there was enough improvement for Miss Dalgleish to feel justified in taking it away.

But what Lilli found hardest to abandon was her free-ranging scavenging which had always been to her what the wide open prairie must have been to an American cowboy. She went on scavenging because Miss Dalgleish couldn't stop her, but what was the point of it?

I was already asleep one night on the verandah (where my bed was) when I was nudged awake by Lilli who knew everything that went on around the four walls of almost every house in town.

'Wake up, Kit,' she whispered. 'I've got something for you.'

'What?' I groaned sleepily, sitting up.

'Look,' she said and dumped a sugarbag on the bed. The bag moved. Something living was in it.

'Take it away,' I said. 'It's a cat.'

'No it isn't, it's two rabbits.'

'Rabbits!' In a country (an entire continent) that was overrun by rabbits nothing seemed more senseless than putting two live rabbits in a sugarbag to deliver to a friend in the middle of the night.

'You're crazy,' I said. 'I don't want them.'

'But they're different.'

In fact the Dunoons, who lived at the other end of town, had an esoteric taste for Belgian hares which was always laughed at in the town, and Lilli had acquired two of them from their hutch on the Dunoon verandah. But she had nowhere to go with them. She couldn't take them home to

Miss Dalgleish or Mrs Peters, and though I was flattered to be trusted by Lilli with a cold-blooded offer of loot I said I didn't want them.

'They'll only ask me where I got them and they'll know they're from the Dunoons. Put them back,' I advised her.

Lilli could never return a valuable prize so she set them free on the river bank where they were caught two days later by Mr Snowdon's greyhounds and killed. And the mystery of it was—if the Stubecks had left town, who had stolen them from the Dunoon's verandah? Lilli was suspected, but it seemed illogical. So much so that she had her defenders, including my mother, who refused to believe it was Lilli.

'She's with Miss Dalgleish now. She doesn't need to steal,' my mother said, and though I knew different I was pleased that my mother defended Lilli and I agreed with her.

'If they go on blaming Lilly every time something is missing,' I said, 'they might as well put her in prison without even trying her.'

'Nonetheless . . .' my father said.

He knew who had stolen those hares. So did the Dunoons. They telephoned Miss Dalgleish and accused Lilli, and though Miss Dalgleish defended her, she nonetheless questioned her about it.

'Did you steal those hares, Lilli?' she asked as she stood Lilli before her in the library, the place where they now held their most formal communications.

'No,' Lilli said.

'Are you sure?'

'Positive.'

'All right, I'll tell Mrs Dunoon again that you had nothing to do with it. I knew you didn't, and I told her so.'

Lilli was disappointed. Why didn't Miss Dalgleish persist so that she could own up? Lying first and admitting guilt afterwards was no more than a convention with Lilli, because it was pointless admitting anything without being forced to. And on the whole she preferred the truth.

'I took them' she said as Miss Dalgleish wrote something in her little black book.

'Oh no, Lilli. Not after what I just said.'

'They were only rabbits,' Lilli said.

'But why? You don't need to steal any more.'

'It's not stealing,' Lilli argued. 'The Dunoons've got hundreds of rabbits.'

'It doesn't matter how many they've got. In fact they were not rabbits at all. They were valuable Belgian hares. But it makes no difference. You had no right to take them.'

'I only took two.'

'But why, Lilli? What for?'

Lilli was trapped. Ask mushroom fanatics why they hunt mushrooms, gold seekers why they hunt gold, golfers why they knock a little ball around a golf course; none of these comparisons occurred to Lilli but her defence of herself (for herself) was made of the same stuff.

'You can't stop me,' she said defiantly.

'But I have to, Lilli. You simply can't go on with your old ways.'

'You can't stop me,' Lilli said again.

'Oh, yes I can. And I will.'

'How?'

Miss Dalgleish pushed Lilli into a chair and stood over her. 'By showing you how senseless it is. You're not a thief, Lilli, not really. But what you have to do is make yourself *understand* that you're not a thief. That's all.'

'Everybody takes things,' Lilli pointed out.

'Even if everybody takes things, which I dispute, it's no reason why you should. In fact you know very well that you don't do things because other people do them, it's not your character. So that's no excuse.'

Lilli was nonplussed. She had expected moral judgments, instead she was getting a quick lesson in her own philosophy from someone who seemed to understand it, even though she disagreed with it.

'What are you going to do about the rabbits?' Lilli said, trying to divert Miss Dalgleish from any more dangerous insight.

'I shall pay the Dunoons for the rabbits and apologise on your behalf.' Miss Dalgleish looked very closely at

Lilli as if seeking something she hadn't yet found. 'I don't suppose you would apologise to them if I asked you to, would you?'

'What would you want me to say?'

'That you did it on the spur of the moment, which I think is true, and that you won't do it again.'

'I'm not going to say anything like that,' Lilli said defiantly. 'I don't like the Dunoons.'

'Then I'll say it for you, Lilli. You are not going to escape the truth. I shan't let you.'

'Can I go now?' Lilli asked.

'Yes. But look at your uniform.'

Lilli's new tunic already had a small tear in the back pleat and an ink stain on the belt: a condition that Lilli thought perfectly normal.

'Take your tunic off and I'll sew it for you. I don't suppose you can sew, can you?' Miss Dalgleish said.

'No.'

'Then I'll have to teach you. Give the belt to Mrs Peters tomorrow and get into your blue dress and bring your homework to me.'

'I haven't got any homework.'

'Oh, yes you have. Bring me your books.'

Education to Lilli had always been a secret process. She was too bright to be ignorant, but she refused to cooperate with teachers, so that whatever she learned she considered nobody's business but her own. In the elementary classes teachers had given up trying to teach Lilli anything. She was a gypsy, and knowing what her home conditions were and her reputation teachers didn't expect her to do homework or even learn by rote the lessons she was set. On the whole (apart from her first year with Boom) she was simply left alone and ignored, so that nobody really knew how much Lilli was taking in, except that it was just enough to lift her year by year into the next class.

But it was different at High School. There were different teachers for different subjects and each teacher had his or her own ideas about Lilli, so that some of them (English, French, History and Drawing) expected Lilli to be up to standard, whereas others (Science, Maths and Geography) expected little or nothing. But all of them demanded a minimum as well as some sort of attempt at homework, and Miss Dalgleish knew it. She had walked in her mincing step, bag over her arm, a parasol in her hand up the hill to the High School to speak with the headmaster and the head woman teacher, so she knew approximately what was expected of Lilli. It meant that Lilli was now forced to expose herself, to reveal to Miss Dalgleish how much she knew or didn't know, and Miss Dalgleish was not going to be very compromising when it came to school work.

'I can't help you much with mathematics or science,' she told Lilli, 'but I can help with the other subjects. Moreover you will do extra French and English with me, and I expect you to be serious about it.'

She set some rules for Lilli to follow. 'After school,' she said, 'you must go straight home and come straight to me in the library where we will decide each evening what you will study. Your homework must come first, and though I shan't keep you in all the time, you must finish that before you do anything else. After that you can read or listen to the gramophone or do whatever else I will set for you.'

So Lilli had to produce her English and French books and admit that she had an English composition and a French conjugation to do. 'My Summer Holidays' was the subject for her composition, and Miss Dalgleish told her that it should be very easy for her. 'You can write about the river and swimming,' she said, 'and eating tomatoes from Mr Hislop's field. Everything you did. And I want a full page, Lilli, not the half page you did last time. Now what conjugation do you have?'

Lilli refused to say a word in French so she pointed to the verb Parler in her textbook: present tense.

'Parler!' Miss Dalgleish said as if she were plucking a small and lovely flower; and she went on plucking flowers as she said in perfect French, 'Je parle, Tu parles, Il parle, Nous parlons, Vous parlez, Ils parlent. It's so simple. So write it out and then you can recite it to me.'

Lilli had been given a small desk of her own in the library and as she sat down to write her composition she asked herself in Stubeck language why she was doing it.

There was nothing to stop her getting up and climbing the wall and finding her way back to the river. Of all the changes in her life she missed the river most, particularly at this time of the day when school was over and when at home she would have had every reason to keep away from Matty and her mother. There was always the marvellous river, even when it was too high and fast to swim in.

'You've got to do it, Lilli,' she heard Miss Dalgleish say to her. 'So just pick up your pen and get on with it.'

'I'm thinking,' Lilli said.

'No you're not. You're daydreaming.'

Lilli took up her pen and in five minutes she had finished half a page of: 'In summer we always go swimming at The Point. I went every day. Sometimes twice a day. We always play around and duck each other. We throw mud at each other. We don't like it when we have to go home . . .' Etc., etc.

When she had finished she pushed it across the table towards Miss Dalgleish who said: 'No. Get up and bring it to me.'

Lilli did as she was told and stood still and silent in front of Miss Dalgleish until she had finished reading the composition. 'This isn't a composition,' Miss Dalgleish said. 'It's a series of silly facts. A composition not only has to describe what you do but what it feels like to do it. You must say what it's like to walk down to the river in your bare feet, avoiding the thorns. Then what it's like when you dive in, and what you feel when you are swimming and playing. The feel of the water. Then a little about the river—how it is low and calm in summer and high and fast in winter, and how sad you are when you can't swim any more. That's what a composition is, Lilli, so please do it again, and a full page.'

But it was more than enough for Lilli.

'You can't make me,' she said in her cat's voice and Lilli was out through the library door and over the wall before Miss Dalgleish could get up from her chair.

It was still daylight and Lilli ran through the main street and along the side streets to the river where she flopped down exhausted. Then she dawdled along the bank putting markers on the water's edge so that she could check the height of the river next day. She skipped stones across the stream and plaited willow fronds around her legs and finally she went into the house on The Point, deserted now and still piled high with the dirty newspapers and the kitchen rubbish the Stubecks had left behind.

Lilli found nothing here to be sentimental about, not even the broken piano stool which had finally lost a leg. She had once hidden a box of matches behind a loose brick in the tilted chimney. She went outside and found the matches and filled the old stove with newspaper and wood and lit it.

'Everybody'll see the smoke,' she said aloud, 'and wonder who's moved in.'

Having tricked the town she knew it was time to go 'home' because it was almost dark. Despite Lilli's courage in almost everything else she was afraid to be alone in the dark along the river bank; she believed in river ghosts; so she left the river by the quickest route and drifted back to the high wooden wall of the Dalgleish manor. She scrambled up the side of the wall and sat on top for a moment to look in wonder at the big house under the old gum trees, sunk in its lush garden, lit by electric lights. And from somewhere inside she heard the sound of passionate singing, a man singing.

'She's playing the gramophone,' Lilli said and dangled her legs over the wall as she listened to Enrico Caruso singing *Vieni sul mar*.

Lilli had no intention of sneaking into the house. She slid down the wall and opened the kitchen door and was frying herself two eggs when Miss Dalgleish came into the kitchen. Lilli waited for a slap or a push, a censure of some kind for her wickedness. For a moment they stood there looking at each other like turtles in their shells.

'What are you doing, Lilli?'

'Frying an egg,' Lilli said.

'Your supper is in the icebox.'

'I want an egg.'

'You can't live on fried eggs.'

'I don't like cold meat and lettuce and all that stuff.'

'It's better for you.'

Miss Dalgleish took the frying pan from the wood stove and tipped the eggs into the dustbin. 'And when you have finished your supper come into the library and finish your homework.'

'I've finished it.'

'No, you haven't. I shan't make you do your composition again because I was wrong to be so brutal with it. Next time you have a composition we'll have to discuss it before you start. So you must do your French and then you can listen to the gramophone.'

Lilli loved the gramophone, no matter what record Miss Dalgleish put on it, but knowing it was not a bribe, knowing it was part of Miss Dalgleish's instruction, she was not going to admit any interest in it, any more than she was normally willing to admit the truth before she had to.

'Where did you go?' Miss Dalgleish asked her.

'To The Point.'

'Next time you run off like that, change your clothes first.' Miss Dalgleish put on her pince-nez and suddenly saw Lilli's real condition. 'Good heavens look at you.'

Lilli's uniform was covered in mud smears, so were her shoes and stockings. Her hands were black from the old wooden stove at The Point, and her face was smudged with soot.

'Don't you dare touch anything in this house before you have washed your face and hands,' Miss Dalgleish said, losing her temper. 'Go and do it now and take your shoes and stockings off and leave them in the bathroom.'

Finally relieved of a burden without knowing quite what it was, Lilli went into the bathroom and began to sing in a very loud voice *O vieni sul mar* but she sang the words that her father had always used: 'Two lovely black eyes, Oh what a surprise, Only for telling a man he was wrong, Two lovely black eyes . . .'

I have my own memory of Lilli at this particular time and it left me with a question that would take years to answer. Miss Dalgleish gave Lilli the choice of eating at home or making up her own lunch and taking it to school.

One day I saw her eating the lunch she had prepared herself. It was cold fried egg smothered with tomato sauce and sandwiched between two thick pieces of white buttered bread.

'How can you eat it?' I said to her.

'It's lovely,' she said. 'My favourite.'

She had a fried egg sandwich day after day until one day she brought instead a couple of modest meat sandwiches with tomato and cucumber slices in them, obviously made by someone else. She disposed of the sliced tomato and cucumber, and ate the meat.

'What happened to the fried egg and tomato sauce?' I asked her.

'They won't let me have it. Miss Dalgleish took away the tomato sauce even though it was my own bottle. It didn't belong to her.'

'Where did you get it?' I said.

'I bought it,' she said.

I knew what that meant, and a couple of days later she was still eating the modest meat sandwiches but she had soaked them in tomato sauce.

'Did she give it back?' I asked her.

'No. I got another bottle and hid it,' she said. 'I love tomato sauce, Kit. I could live on it.'

I watched Lilli wolfing her sandwiches and licking her fingers, and though I was no older than she was I had enough curiosity or perhaps it was imagination to wonder even then how Lilli was ever going to be fitted into Miss Dalgleish's life. Lilli's tunic, stockings, blouse and shoes were of the finest quality that Williams the draper's could supply, but she wore her clothes more like a prison uniform than a school uniform. She made no awesome concession at all to her sudden change in circumstances, and I knew that Lilli and Miss Dalgleish were measuring each other every day, as if to see who would finally win.

# 8

WHAT WE SAW OF THE RELATIONSHIP FROM THE OUTSIDE WAS its effect on Lilli, because she was always among us—at school, on the river, in the town. We saw most of it by incidence. We knew how strict Miss Dalgleish was with Lilli, and we knew (because we could see) that Lilli survived it. What we didn't see was its effect on Miss Dalgleish, at least not until the very end when it was too late. So we never did know what went on between them day after day, week after week as Miss Dalgleish tried to make Lilli over into the thing she wanted, while Lilli stubbornly resisted but at the same time became a different person.

Miss Dalgleish must have known that she would have to allow for a sentiment she couldn't provide herself, and also for another kind of response that was vital to a girl like Lilli. So she bought Lilli a Scotch terrier named Tilley.

Tilley became, in fact, a copy of Lilli. He was a tough little dog, utterly loyal and devoted to his mistress. But he was so independent that he became a figure in the town in his own right because he frequently escaped from the Dalgleish fortress during the day and roamed the streets on his short legs, tipping over dustbins, chasing the cats, taking instant likes and dislikes to certain people and, when friendly, expressing it with a certain restrained dignity that asked no forgiveness for his wickedness. He was never mean, and he only bit those people who aimed a kick at him; which included Jack South the painter, Joe Collins the police sergeant, Dorman Walker the feed and grain merchant and Mr Howland the chemist. He never touched children, and though they all wanted to make friends with him he was inclined to keep his distance. He looked in on churches, the court, the shire hall and once or twice turned up at school to the delight of everybody in it except Lilli, who took him home in disgrace. When he was with Lilli he was obedient, wary and respectable, but it was all a deception for Lilli's sake. He went swimming with her, would dive in with the rest of us, and though he would face up bravely to bigger dogs he would always turn tail and run if he was caught in a backyard; and he knew almost every front and backyard in town. Knowing the dog, we also knew Lilli.

Lilli at school was mostly the girl we already knew, and though she was physically and visually and actively the same person, the curious emergence of Lilli as a clever girl was almost imperceptible. She never did cooperate with the teachers, and if she learned anything it seemed to be because she chose to and not because a teacher had captured her interest. As a result she remained an enigma to all teachers who rather resented her independence, yet they began to respect her intelligence and tried to help her despite herself. What they didn't realise perhaps was that every night in the library at Miss Dalgleish's there was a parallel education going on which stimulated Lilli's intelligence, so that she was quick to learn what teachers had to teach her. Perhaps that was part of Miss Dalgleish's plan, but though her French and English and History began to show results that were more than satisfactory, she never volunteered any of her information in class. Asked, she would reply—briefly and to the point. But she would never add anything, and I don't remember her ever asking a question.

When it became obvious that Lilli had become an avid reader, our English teacher, Miss Yardley, who now took a special interest in Lilli, tried to discover exactly what books she was reading in Miss Dalgleish's library but, failing to make any headway with Lilli, Miss Yardley called on Miss Dalgleish to find out for herself. Seeing the library, and hearing Miss Dalgleish's report, she made the mistake of saying in class next day:

'Lilli: I know you have just read two books by Henry

Handel Richardson. Would you kindly tell the class what they were about and what you thought of them?'

'How do you know I read them?' Lilli demanded.

'I asked Miss Dalgleish.'

'You've got no right,' Lilli said.

'But I was interested in your progress, Lilli, so I called on Miss Dalgleish because I want to know what you are reading. After all, the subject is English.'

Lilli normally got on well with Miss Yardley and was never rude to her, but the idea of anyone calling on Miss Dalgleish to ask questions about her, any question, was anathema. If Lilli guarded Miss Dalgleish's secrets, she obviously expected her own to be respected. She wanted no one to know what she did behind that wooden wall.

'Miss Dalgleish has no right either,' she said to Miss Yardley. 'It's nothing to do with you what I do at home, Miss Yardley.'

'I'm sorry, Lilli, but I wasn't prying I assure you.'

Nonetheless Miss Yardley never repeated the visit and, though Lilli didn't mention it in her black book, there was obviously a quarrel between herself and Miss Dalgleish about it, because Miss Dalgleish walked up the hill to the school a few days later and was closeted with Miss Yardley and some of the other teachers. Thereafter no teacher ever asked Lilli what she did behind those high wooden walls.

In fact we never really discovered what Lilli and Miss Dalgleish considered fair or unfair to each other, or even how they managed to match their different moralities. Nobody (not even Dorothy Malone) ever heard their arguments about morality, but they did have them, and since at the time the only universal instruction in what was right and wrong, good or evil, was from the pulpit, the moment came when Miss Dalgleish decided it was time that Lilli joined the rest of us in getting some instruction in the proper place.

I don't think Lilli knew what religion, or rather what sect she belonged to, but Miss Dalgleish, of Scottish origin, was a Presbyterian, and one Sunday morning she walked through the town with Lilli beside her on the way to church. Lilli wore a neat cotton dress, black patent leather shoes, a blazer, a boater and short white gloves.

I was on my way to church with my brother Tom and I couldn't keep the surprise out of my voice as I greeted Lilli and Miss Dalgleish.

'Are you going to church, Kit?' Miss Dalgleish said.

It was a superfluous question because we were in our best Sunday clothes. 'Yes, Miss Dalgleish,' I said.

'Good. Then you can accompany us,' she said.

'But we don't go to the Presbyterian Church,' I pointed out. 'We're Church of England at the moment.' (My father allowed us to choose our own church.)

'Oh, of course,' Miss Dalgleish said. She wore a large-brimmed hat, a long, soft, black, silk gown edged with fine lace, and her jet beads glittered in the sun. 'In any case,' she said, 'would you mind coming with us today so that Lilli doesn't feel too strange?'

Only Miss Dalgleish could have asked someone to change sects in the middle of the main street on a Sunday morning.

'I'm all right,' Lilli protested.

It was Tom, the moralist in the family, who said. 'We don't mind, Miss Dalgleish.'

'I'm sure you don't, Tom, but will your parents mind?' Miss Dalgleish said as an afterthought.

'I don't think so,' I said, so we went into the ugly little iron-roofed Presbyterian Church and sat six rows from the front with every eye in the church on us, and a lot of whispered comment all around us.

'What do we do, Kit?' Lilli asked.

'I don't know,' I said.

Lilli knew nothing about the routine of any service, and I wasn't sure what happened in a Presbyterian church. But I do remember the sermon that day because as far as Lilli was concerned it was directed personally at her. The Minister, the Reverend Armitage, was a tiny Scot who had to stand on a fruit box to be seen over the pulpit, but his voice was loud and harsh, and though he began his sermon with a text from Corinthians which said, 'We are made as filth of the world and are the offscouring of all things unto this day', it became very quickly a denunciation of what was happening to our young men and women. There had been a spate of petty thefts in the town, obviously some of our unemployed youths on the rampage, so on the one hand he directed his anger at theft, scavenging, and property violation, and on the other hand he denounced the nakedness and looseness of our young girls who went to the swimming hole half-naked and cavorted there with boys, even on the Sabbath, which Lilli had always done.

'Don't take any notice of him,' I whispered to Lilli.

'I'm not,' she said.

She refused to sing, although I don't think she knew the hymns anyway, and when it was time for the collection she refused to put in the shilling that Miss Dalgleish had given her, though Miss Dalgleish said: 'Put your money on the plate, Lilli.'

'Not me,' Lilli said.

I thought at the end of the service that Lilli would never be seen in a church again, so I was surprised the next Sunday when she was waiting alone for Tom and me outside the big wooden gate and dressed for church.

'I'm coming with you,' she said to me.

'I'm not going back to the Presbyterians,' I pointed out.

'No. I'll try yours, Kit. Maybe it's better.'

It was not something that was quite accepted in our town—for a boy and girl of our age to walk to church together unless there was an adult between them, but whereas I was embarrassed, Lilli didn't care. So we walked into the Church of England at the other end of town, and once again all eyes were on us. This time it wasn't so bad because the sermon was something about hope and charity, but when it came to prayers Lilli refused to kneel.

'Get down,' I said.

'Not me,' she whispered.

It was nothing to do with a libertarian attitude, it was simply that Lilli knew she would look silly and out of character kneeling in prayer. There was a lot more whispering, and someone from behind nudged her in the back, but Lilli remained upright in the pew.

I didn't see Lilli the next Sunday but I heard that she had tried the Methodists. The logical place for Lilli was probably the Catholic Church because her friend Dorothy Malone was a Catholic, but Catholicism was too absolute for Lilli, and anyway the barriers of religion were so strong in our town that even Lilli didn't attempt to breach them. She was not a Catholic; she knew that much.

Church-going was the price she had to pay for her free Sunday afternoons with Dorothy Malone, and though thereafter she didn't go to church every Sunday, we would meet her from time to time in the Church of England which she seemed to have settled for, simply because of its evangelical weakness and its lack of thunder. But she never did kneel to pray, she never sang, and she never put a penny in the collection box. In fact Lilli remained what she had always been—a natural heathen with a coda of curious superstitions; west winds gave you spots, jumping fish were bad luck, eight magpies were good luck, if you heard dogs barking when you were eating you got a stomach ache, and horses that defecated noisily gave you TB if you touched their hindquarters. There were dozens more.

Eventually Miss Dalgleish settled for what she could get, which was that occasional visit to the Church of England. But she did insist that Lilli read the Bible, which Lilli said she enjoyed.

'I don't think she knows what's in it,' Lilli said to me one Sunday.

I could imagine what Lilli had found in the Bible, apart from the marvellous stories that were told in the sort of language that suited her. But I don't think she found religion in it because she didn't look for it, and to the very end she denied all formal religion because there was another root to Lilli's beliefs.

It was this other aspect of Lilli's heterodoxy that told me something about her secret sensibilities. Our town was surrounded by wheat fields, orange groves, vineyards, a rich valley and a long line of gum trees that fringed the river banks of both our rivers, for we had two: the Little Murray and the Big Murray with an island between them.

Sounds were as indigenous to our surroundings as the gum trees and the oranges and the wheat, and in summer you could sit on the back step of the house and hear the town breathing and the voices of children playing in sandy backyards—distant summer voices. As the summer evening came over us like a soft mauve cloud from the warm sky, the dogs would bark and you could hear the crickets from across the river slowly giving way to the dull, gasping thunder of a million bullfrogs. I loved to hear the day coming to its end, and I thought I was the only person in town who heard it that way until Lilli said to me as we were the last to leave The Point one evening:

'Have you ever heard the tomato plants closing up for the night, Kit?'

'What do you mean—heard them?'

'Well just listen for a moment.'

We were standing in the middle of Mr Hislop's tomato plantations: five acres of them between the river and the railway line, and far enough from the centre of the town for the evening to be still and quiet.

'Only you have to squat,' Lilli said.

I joined Lilli, squatting on my haunches and listening very carefully.

'I can't hear anything,' I said.

'Shhh . . . just listen,' she said.

I listened again and this time I heard a curious mosaic of sounds, a tiny silken rustle all around me as if a thousand little movements were taking place, so soft that if the evening had not been deathly still I couldn't have heard anything.

'It's the leaves curling up,' she said. 'It's the same early morning, only then it's rather scratchy.'

'I'll be damned,' I said.

'Some gum trees do it too,' she told me. 'You can hear the bark closing up, only you have to catch it at the right moment.'

'How did you find out?' I said.

'I don't know,' she replied. 'I just heard it one day. You can hear a lot of things if you put your ear to the ground at eventide. All sorts of noises.'

I realised then that Lilli had her feet deep in the earth, on the asphalt, in the mud: she was firmly rooted to the stuff underneath and, like an ancient Greek, there was a presence in it to a God unknown.

That was something that Miss Dalgleish couldn't change or influence, but what she did do for Lilli was to transform her language and to some extent even her accent. Lilli's speech was always blunt and remained so, but Miss Dalgleish over a period of time managed by repeated correction to persuade Lilli to say 'I don't know' instead of 'I dunno'; 'I'm sure' for 'You bet'; and in one extraordinary transformation 'Grab him' became 'Seize him'. 'Grab' was a common word to all of us—but Miss Dalgleish hated it, and after two years of correcting Lilli the day came at The Point when Lilli actually called out 'Seize him' when someone was running away and had to be stopped in a game we were playing. We laughed, but we liked it and adopted it ourselves. But whereas Lilli used it seriously, we used it in fun. She didn't deliberately drop her slang expressions, they seemed slowly to disappear, and in one other aspect of language she became an authority for us—French.

Our French teacher for one term was a Frenchman named Monsieur Henri Danjou. The entire school called him Henri because he was a foreigner and therefore a little ridiculous so we were perfectly justified in being familiar. He was short and stocky and he rode a French racing bike with light wooden wheels and a razor-like seat. He was made fun of not only by his pupils but by half the adults in town as well, so that his life became a daily battle to survive the mockery of his thick accent, plus a dozen other teasing provocations from children and adults. Over the months he narrowed his response to a French expression we believed to be 'Visez mon cou' translated as 'Aim at my neck' which we took to be a flabby French insult. It was Lilli who told us that we were stupid.

'He's saying "Baisez mon cul" which means kiss my arse,' she said.

We collapsed. If some of the other girls who were good at French knew what it was, it was only Lilli who had the

courage to tell us, and thereafter we respected Monsieur
Danjou for his ability, in the Australian idiom, to stand
up for himself and give as good as he got. It explains why
Lilli told us what he was saying. She wanted his version of
it known without herself taking sides for she hated to see
others mocked. She never mocked anyone herself, and
she allowed no one to be mocked to her, which was not an
easy discipline to follow, because in Australia at that time
mockery and ridicule were almost a cultural activity. In
any case it was all too much for Monsieur Danjou. He
disappeared with his bicycle at the end of term and we
never heard of him again, although his French response
to our teasing became part of local lore, thanks to Lilli.

Though she rarely criticised anyone, Lilli had her likes
and dislikes in the town and she made them known. Just
as Miss Dalgleish always seemed to know what was going
on in the town, Lilli always seemed to know who had
laughed at her behind her back and who supported her,
or at least left her alone. Most people had long ago learned
that they would get the worst of it if they ever ridiculed
Lilli to her face. She still settled accounts, no matter how
long it took and, as a result, much of what was said behind
Lilli's back was often exaggerated.

I once heard Bob Summerfield, a local motorbike
enthusiast and an early womaniser who must have seen
something in Lilli that he was hoping to find there—I
once heard Bob claim that he had seen Lilli, aged fourteen,
smoking behind the Chinese Laundry. The combination
was too much. For a woman to be seen smoking in our
town placed her in a special category, for someone to do it
behind the Chinese Laundry suggested all kind of evil
addictions, and finally for a fourteen year old schoolgirl
to do it was wickedness itself.

I didn't dispute the statement because I never interfered,
and I knew that Lilli would take care of it anyway. She
soon heard it, and what she resented was not so much the
silly suggestiveness of it, but the fact that Bob Summerfield
should talk about her behind her back. If she wanted to
smoke behind the Chinese Laundry Lilli would do it
openly, but in fact it was a lie, and Bob was going to suffer
for it. He had a beautifully kept BSA motorbike with an

acetylene lighting system, and one morning he discovered that the acetylene holder of the lamp had been unscrewed and the acetylene crystals had been tipped into the petrol tank.

Bob knew who had done it and he complained to Miss Dalgleish, who then tackled Lilli with it. Lilli said of course she had done it and explained why. As a result Miss Dalgleish told Bob he was a very silly man.

'Lilli doesn't do things in holes and corners,' she said to Bob, 'and it is wicked of you to suggest it.'

'Ah . . . I was only joking,' Bob said lamely.

'Then you ought to know that it's foolish to joke about Lilli. I have no sympathy for you at all.'

'She's ruined my bike,' Bob said angrily. 'She's spoiled the tank.'

'It's your own fault,' Miss Dalgleish insisted.

'Well two can play at that game,' he said.

'I wouldn't advise it,' Miss Dalgleish told him. 'And if you spread any more scandal about Lilli I'll bring you to court for defamation. Even one word.'

Bob knew when he was beaten. The combination of primitive threats from Lilli and rich and powerful ones from Miss Dalgleish were too much for him, and he kept his mouth shut thereafter and got himself a new petrol tank.

If Miss Dalgleish was loyal to Lilli, so Lilli was to her. I don't think anyone in the town ever dared criticise or mock Miss Dalgleish in front of Lilli but occasionally someone would try to question Lilli about Miss Dalgleish. At first Lilli's replies would be evasive, then they usually turned rude. We had one busybody named Mrs Ellis, a religious sentimentalist who like to 'help', and she told Lilli she ought to be more considerate towards Miss Dalgleish.

'I notice that you still call her Miss Dalgleish, Lilli. Why don't you call her Auntie?'

'Because she's not my aunt,' Lilli said.

'I know. But I'm sure she would like it if you did.'

'You don't know anything about it,' Lilli said with a contemptuous little laugh.

Mrs Ellis was lucky that Lilli considered her harmless

rather than vicious, but that little laugh was a comment. Lilli rarely laughed, and if she smiled it was always slight and fleeting. In fact her mouth was the most disciplined part of her rather free swinging body. She had bold eyes, deft hands and lively, lovely hair, but the only time I remember her smiling freely was with Dorothy Malone and with Tilley her dog, and sometimes with me when we were alone. Otherwise the smile was rare and disciplined.

And that was how Lilli was growing up.

# 9

BY THE TIME SHE WAS FIFTEEN, LILLI HAD BECOME AN IMPORTANT girl in our school because she was by then one of our cleverest girls. She was also one of our most cultured girls, if only because she had an excellent library at her disposal and she loved to read; and because some of Miss Dalgleish's taste in music and art became her taste. The curious thing is that we all knew this about Lilli, yet apart from her school work we never saw Lilli reading a book or listening to music. It was something we simply knew about, and some of our girls were even in awe of Lilli, not because of her old reputation for physical retaliation but for what she secretly knew but never bothered to show.

She was still the same taciturn, threatening Lilli, only now it was more of an invisible threat. She needed retaliation less and less because most of the town had grown to accept her as a true ward of Miss Dalgleish's. They no longer thought of her or treated her as the thieving, scavenging Stubeck she had been when she was with her family. But though Lilli had given up thieving and scavenging it was occasionally reported that she had been seen wandering aimlessly around the town at midnight, sometimes with Tilley, as if every now and then she had to revert to the wide open spaces of the back streets in order to be free in some old anarchic way. She no longer climbed over the wall but walked out through the big gates, and if Miss Dalgleish knew what she was doing she apparently let it pass as a momentary aberration, a backward reversion that wasn't very serious.

What made any scandal about Lilli easy was her attraction for boys and men. Lilli had never been an ugly duckling, she had never even been a tomboy because she had always been very much a girl, even as a scavenging child. At fifteen she was the kind of girl who attracted any boy or man who wanted a challenge. If she was beautiful it was because she had the rather bold eyes of an animal, a rather stern brow and a perfect body that was utterly lacking in self-consciousness. She moved her body carelessly, sometimes recklessly, and any man who wanted to be conquered would look at Lilli with the thought that here was something worth capturing, if you could get it—and Lilli's reserve made the challenge a real one. She had never looked innocent. By now men were beginning to treat her as if she would abandon her innocence without question if she wanted to. There was no fear in her, no shrinking, no coyness, and certainly no guile in her femininity. So our most sexually ambitious men took this as an enticement.

There were of course all kinds of boys and men in our town: the soft and the hard, the gentle and the ruthless, but whereas the soft and gentle ones were defeated by Lilli before they had even tried to make up to her, the hard and the ruthless among us were the heroes in this sort of situation. It was already said of Lilli that she needed someone to show her what was what, so we were supposed to admire the kind of man who would do it. Yet only two men tried to show Lilli what was what. One was Tod (Theodore) Dorking, a sixteen year old schoolboy, and the other was Phillip Anstee, our local land and estate agent.

Tod was as popular and extrovert as Lilli was secretive and rather isolated. The school was proud of Tod because he was a fairly good scholar, a marvellous footballer and a Victorian junior swimming champion. He was tall, inclined to bigness and early fatness, but blessed with the kind of masculine face and leaning sort of thick body that would, in manhood, make him the ideal Australian. But though we all liked Tod we knew there was a cold streak in him which, in football, flattened you with a legal bump so professionally done that it was planned to cause maximum damage. Tod would often pick you up from a heap but he would always laugh and say: 'You should have seen that one coming.' With Tod you could never see it coming; he made sure you didn't.

With Lilli he was cautious and good-natured. Though we remembered him as a very conventional and well-behaved little boy, he tried to show Lilli that he too had been something of a tearaway when he was ten or eleven, stealing (he said) oranges and pomegranates from the Smith's place, opening the chicken coop doors at the Dawson's place, and cutting down a neighbour's hedge with a tomahawk. None of it was true but he was telling Lilli that it didn't matter if she had been a thief and a scavenger. He had been one himself. Lilli listened impassively to all this, because she would always listen, but the more reluctant she was the more elaborate were Tod's efforts to ingratiate himself, not by being friendly but always with some proof of his roughness and villainy, as if that was the way to Lilli's heart.

The mistake Tod made was to believe that he was succeeding. So much so that at a school social held one night at the end of term he tried to kiss Lilli. They were among four or five others (including myself) who were outside the assembly hall on one of the raised corridors that ran around the courtyard of the school. We used to sit on the iron railing and swing our legs, and that is what we were doing as we listened to a girl named Marjorie Rankin playing the piano inside. Eventually only Tod and Lilli were left in a dark corner, Tod for his own reasons and Lilli because she was caught for a moment by Marjorie Rankin's very good performance. But suddenly Tod pushed his hand around her neck.

'What about it, Lilli?' he said.

'What about what?' she asked.

'You know what,' Tod said.

'No I don't,' Lilli told him.

'You're only saying that,' Tod said and, pulling Lilli roughly off the railing, he put his arms around her, held her, and tried to kiss her. The struggle was seen by four of us who had re-emerged to join them. Though it was dark I saw Lilli bunch herself up like a tiger before she sprang on Tod. She got a grip on Tod's short hair, pushed his head back so that he was bent over the railing, and then tipped him right over the railing to the ground. It was all over in a second and Tod was lying in the gravel below. We all laughed, but I saw Lilli's teeth literally flash.

'What did he do?' the girls asked.

Lilli walked inside and said, 'Nothing.'

The whole school knew about it next day, and a day later so did the whole town. But it reflected on Lilli rather than Tod. Tod was a popular, respectable, athletic boy, and if there was any kind of boy and girl trouble between him and Lilli then it was obviously Lilli's fault. This was the sort of situation when some of the town remembered where Lilli had come from and what she had been. In an incident so primitive and adolescent and funny most of the town would normally have laughed it off, but never when Lilli was concerned, even now, and she had to suffer for it.

The Phillip Anstee affair was different, yet it had the same result. Anstee was in his early thirties, a successful land and estate agent who looked exactly what he was—the handsome remnant of some English aristocratic family that had long ago dissipated itself in self-destruction. His face was rather cadaverous, but with good cheekbones, a strong nose and bright blue eyes. He was a cold, self-possessed man, a gentleman—albeit now an Australian one. His Australian wife was older than he was by about eight years and we all knew that he had come into the town ten years before and set up his land and estate agency on his wife's money. She was pink and blonde, and what had once been a full Venusian figure was now turning into a matronly blowzy, plumpness. The town also knew that Anstee took his pleasures where he could find them. Much later when I was able to hear such things he was reported to favour happily-married women, as if that was the sort of challenge he needed to justify his infidelities. But more often than not his work took him to outlying districts where wives were hardworking, lonely, and often neglected. A farmer's wife was said never to be safe with Anstee calling for business reasons.

Anstee finally went a little too far with the wife of

Johnny Sullivan who ran a rather isolated citrus grove
near Nooah. Johnny gave Anstee a beating in the middle
of St Helen's main street and then sent his unfaithful wife
packing. Anstee came out of it as a masculine joke, a
known ladies' man (and good luck to him) but foolish
enough to be caught. His wife thought otherwise, and
having put up with his peccadilloes for years she decided
to divorce him.

What was interesting in this quarrel for our family was
that first of all Mrs Anstee approached my father to ask
him to conduct her case, and when he refused (he wouldn't
touch divorce cases) Anstee himself tried to persuade him
to take up the defence, but again my father refused. I
don't know whether my father was influenced or not by
the evidence which Mrs Anstee must have shown him, but
I like to think he was because when the case was heard,
among the evidence presented for her was a diary she had
found in which Anstee had listed his conquests. What was
particularly shocking (and made my father furious when
it was published) was a series of references to Lilli Stubeck.

What he had written about Lilli was not a boast of
conquest but his plans for it. His hopeful descriptions of
Lilli were shameful, and though most of them could not
be published in the local papers the court reports made it
clear that the diary references to our fifteen year old
schoolgirl were so scurrilous that even the judge (Matthews,
R.B.) had stopped counsel reading them out.

Lilli was totally innocent. She wrote in her black book
that she never remembered exchanging a word with Phillip
Anstee, although she had never liked the way he looked at
her. But once again it reflected on Lilli. What was it that a
fifteen year old girl did to a man like Anstee to invoke
such thoughts and plans?

Mrs Anstee got her divorce and almost every other
woman mentioned in the diary was more or less forgotten
but Lilli wasn't. A more fragile girl would have had
difficulty walking through the town after such a scandal,
and in fact it was expected of Lilli that she should show
some shame. But Lilli remained Lilli, and if she saw the
glances or heard the whispers she took no notice of them.

And if men became suddenly interested in this enticing schoolgirl she ignored them, or with a look threatened anyone who would dare say anthing to her—vulgar or sympathetic. It was a situation that Miss Dalgleish could not help her with because it was mostly invisible, and though Miss Dalgleish was as shocked by it as all Lilli's friends were, she too couldn't talk to Lilli about it. Personally I expected and wanted Lilli to burn down Anstee's house, but she didn't retaliate. She had finally grown out of it.

At this time she was on the way to becoming a very attractive young woman who seemed to be more mature than the other girls of her age. She was a self-organised sort of girl with the same old reserve and secret disciplines —the same serious and rather unsmiling and inexplicable Lilli we had always known. And though she was emerging visibly, she didn't seem to be interested in the pleasures it could give her. She came and went from home to school as if that was all her life needed; and in order to be such an excellent student she obviously had to spend hours in Miss Dalgleish's library studying and working. The only childish thing left in Lilli was her handwriting which had remained a large, open-lettered hand that seemed naive until you read what it said; then you realised how un-naive Lilli was.

But where was she going? What was she heading for?

It was a question we often asked about Lilli among ourselves but never asked Lilli herself. Not even Dorothy Malone asked Lilli what would happen at the end of her schooling. Would she stay at home with Miss Dalgleish? Or would Miss Dalgleish send her to Melbourne to University? Obviously she was going to graduate from school with highest honours, and a university education seemed logical, particularly since Miss Dalgleish was one of the few people in our town at that time who could afford it. We couldn't even guess at Lilli's hopes. If she worked hard and well it was simply Lilli being herself. There was never any hint in her manner that there was a final purpose or a serious aim in it, because Lilli would never admit aims.

Moreover we could only guess at what went on at home

although it was fair to assume that her life was so well regulated that she no longer had any serious problems. She still emerged with Miss Dalgleish every Saturday morning, and they would walk silently into town. Lilli still carried the purchases and only occasionally would they exchange a word or two to regulate something. Miss Dalgleish still decided what Lilli should wear and when she should buy it. Almost everything was still bought at Williams, but more often now they went to Miss Thompson's, the dress shop, which had more style and sophistication. Lilli still spent most of her time in school uniform, but when she was not in uniform Miss Dalgleish had her looking smart and at the same time very simple, which suited Lilli. But if Miss Dalgleish was proud of the result she never showed it. It was all practical, down to earth. They still revealed nothing of their relationship, which remained as much a mystery to the town as it had always been.

As for Lilli, she would respond readily and offhandedly to anyone who made a friendly gesture towards her, but always with that inner discipline that held back any real connection. She would talk to any one who wanted to talk to her, but would reply rather than instigate. She was fairly free with friends like Dorothy Malone or myself, or even with some of the teachers who now treated her as a senior, almost as an equal. So she was never quite isolated, never quite alone. Yet she was always on that borderline, and when she went home and closed those big gates behind her we all felt that somewhere inside those walls was Lilli's real life; only we were never quite sure what it was.

I once asked Dorothy Malone if Lilli and Miss Dalgleish still quarrelled.

'I don't really know,' she said.

I knew that Dorothy would not normally discuss what went on in that household, even with me, but I also knew that Dorothy was puzzled and longed to talk to somebody about Lilli, and since I was a trusted friend I didn't mind asking her questions. 'They seem to have regulated their contact so perfectly,' Dorothy said, 'that I doubt if they ever exchange a cross word any more. They're terribly impersonal with each other. They always have been, I know, but I sometimes wonder, Kit, what's going to happen to Lilli.'

'So do I,' I said. 'That's why I asked.'

'There's something there that we don't see,' she said.

'You mean something wrong?'

'Not really. But when I go there I always feel I have to be on Lilli's side in something, although there isn't anything to be on her side about. It's just a feeling I have that I must be loyal to her.'

'You mean Miss Dalgleish criticises her?'

'Never. Oh, I'm probably imagining things. But Lilli still has a secret life somewhere in her, and that's what I'm loyal to, without quite knowing what it is. I always feel I have to be on her side.'

'But you said they don't quarrel.'

'No . . . I said I don't know. Who really knows anything, Kit? In fact it's always been a sort of silent dispute. But you'll see for yourself.'

Dorothy knew that I was going to be invited for afternoon tea on the following Sunday. She said Lilli had told her. But it wasn't Lilli who issued the invitation. It was Miss Dalgleish who rang my mother and asked her if it was all right if I came to 'tea' on Sunday.

'At what time?' my mother asked, wondering why she was being asked on my behalf.

'Five o'clock.'

My mother was a little more confused. Five o'clock 'tea' in Australia meant a proper evening meal, but since that seemed unlikely with Miss Dalgleish it obviously meant afternoon tea in the English manner.

'I'll ask Kit,' my mother said, 'and if it's all right he can tell Lilli.'

'No, please let me know yourself,' Miss Dalgleish said.

'All right.'

My mother was surprised and, as always in any contact with Miss Dalgleish, a little flattered. But she asked me why I thought I had been invited.

'Because I'm polite and respectable and always look as if I've just washed my face and hands,' I said.

'Seriously, Kit. What suddenly brought this on?'

I thought about it for a moment and said, 'I think Miss

Dalgleish feels it's about time Lilli had some contact with boys her own age.'

'But why did she want me to confirm it?'

'She may be afraid that Lilli wants nothing to do with it.'

'Why?'

'Because it's probably Miss Dalgleish's affair, not Lilli's.'

'It seems odd.'

My mother confirmed the acceptance, but I too was surprised when Lilli said to me on the Friday: 'You're coming to tea on Sunday, aren't you?'

'Yes,' I said. 'Miss Dalgleish invited me.'

'I told her to,' Lilli said.

On the Sunday I put on my best suit, polished my shoes and, resisting my mother's suggestion that I take a bunch of her roses with me, I opened the big gates (left unlocked) and walked up the long path between the shrubs and the flowers to the front door. From the moment I entered those gates I was alert to everything around me. The garden of roses, chrysanthemums, rhododendrons and mixed flowerbeds was perfectly kept by the deaf and dumb Bob Andrews, and to one side and at the back there was an orange grove as well as peach trees, apricots, grapefruit, mandarins, plums and vines. One side of the wall had passionfruit and the pomegranates I remembered Lilli acquiring, and the house itself was so unusual for our town that I looked at it as an architectural curiosity. It was brick (most of our houses were wood), had two storeys, leadlight windows on the ground floor, a tiled roof (most of our roofs were corrugated iron), and because the grounds went right through to the next street the house seemed to have two fronts to it.

I heard Tilley bark as I knocked, and then Lilli said 'Be quiet, Tilley' as she opened the old oak door.

'Hello, Lilli,' I said.

'Hello, Kit,' she said. 'Come in.'

She was dressed in a tweed skirt and a Fair Isle jumper which I knew were expensive, but for some curious reason I felt overdressed for Lilli, although I couldn't have worn anything less than a suit.

'Dorothy's here,' she said, but I was too busy inspecting

the house to worry about Dorothy because right there, in the carpeted hall, was one of the naked statues the town loved to scandalise about. It was a small nude of a young woman poised on something like a rock as if she were about to fly up to heaven, her hands grasping her head in what looked like despair. I looked and shrugged it off as Tilley sniffed at my polished shoes and went on growling until Lilli told him again to be quiet.

'He's not used to strangers in here,' she said.

The hall was too dark to see very well but I detected flowers in a vase, a shelf of what I later realised was Venetian glass, and three large unidentifiable pictures on the walls which I knew were abstract and post-impressionist and French.

'Never mind that,' Lilli said to me as I hesitated a moment before them.

'I'm curious,' I whispered.

'Don't waste your time,' she said, and with Tilley's final acceptance (a leap to my hand for a pat) we entered what I assumed to be a salon.

It was a large square room with an oval table at one end already set with a fine damask cloth, china, cutlery, sweets and cakes. The rest of the furniture was solid mahogany: a sideboard, small tables, wing chairs and lamp holders. There were two more nude statues in black granite on little pedestals. There was a Persian carpet on a floor that looked like silk, and above the fireplace hung a large oil painting of old Mr Dalgleish in his high collar. Paintings, photographs and objets d'art covered the walls, and I suppose the ensemble resembled a Victorian-Edwardian drawing room decorated with Art Nouveau.

'Good afternoon, Kit,' Miss Dalgleish said.

'Good afternoon, Miss Dalgleish.'

The French carriage clock on the mantelshelf tingled 5 o'clock and she said, 'You're very prompt, which is admirable at your age. I hate unpunctuality.'

'I had to time it very carefully,' I said and laughed. I was by no means at home, and when I saw Dorothy smiling at me I said, 'Hello Dorothy.'

She simply went on smiling and nodding like a conspirator, and I don't think anybody in our town could smile like Dorothy Malone. It was a greeting and an encouragement which helped me to relax because Dorothy herself was used to this place, whereas I wasn't.

'Sit there,' Miss Dalgleish said and pointed to a heavy Victorian chair. 'It's the only man's chair in the room, and it is where my father used to sit.'

I sank into the monster and watched Lilli and Miss Dalgleish. I had only seen them together in the street, and though it was normal to see them every week without really knowing what they said to each other, or how they behaved inside their wooden walls, that curious tension between them was always obvious, and even two minutes in this house told me that in here they still lived their lives in the same contest: Lilli being determinedly Lilli and Miss Dalgleish exercising only as much control as Lilli would allow. I had expected Lilli to be demure in this place, whereas she flopped down on a couch with her marvellously agile body, and I realised again that after all she was at home here. It was her place.

Miss Dalgleish asked me if my family were well and she said, 'When you leave, Kit, you can take something to your mother for me, so please don't forget.'

'All right,' I said.

She got up then and said, 'Lilli will call me when it's time for tea, so I'll leave you for a little while.'

I stood up.

'Send Tilley in with me, Lilli, so that he doesn't steal the sandwiches,' she said.

'Go on Tilley,' Lilli said to the dog. 'Go inside.'

The dog was at Lilli's feet and she prodded him with her toe. He resisted so she took him by the collar and pushed him after Miss Dalgleish who didn't look back. She opened a door, I caught a glimpse of the library, and when Tilley had followed her in she closed the door and we were left to ourselves.

I was still embarrassed to be here at all but Lilli said: 'Don't look so nervous, Kit. It's only afternoon tea.'

'My mother wondered if it was going to be high tea.'

'Not today,' Lilli said. 'We eat our dinner late on Sundays.'

Normally I would have been a little lost between two

girls but they made it easy because they could talk with me or without me. In fact we had plenty to talk about because our yearly examinations were coming up and we could quarrel about their usefulness. I hated examinations whereas both girls seemed to suck them in like fresh air. After this particular lot of examinations there would be one more year left for all three of us and I knew that Dorothy was easing the conversation into what would happen to us afterwards. It was then that Dorothy told us that she intended to become a nun.

'You a nun?' I said incredulously.

Dorothy was a full-bodied cheerful girl who looked, physically, as if she wanted nothing more than to marry and have children. Her body—the happy poise of it—seemed to invite no other future than quiet motherhood, so that we all thought of Dorothy as the girl who would some day marry one of our decent young men and settle down to a happy future with half a dozen children.

'Yes, me a nun,' Dorothy said, laughing. 'Why not, Kit?'

'I don't know. I just can't picture it.'

It took me no more than a minute to realise that I was wrong. Though Dorothy may have been designed by her God to mother something, she was better fitted for a life of purity and service than any other girl in our town. She would obviously make a perfect nun.

'I always knew you'd do it,' Lilli said to her. 'In fact I can't imagine you being anything else. Ever since I can remember . . .'

'I suppose you're right,' I admitted. 'But when do you have to go?'

'The end of next year,' Dorothy said. 'When I've finished school.'

'What does your mother say?' Lilli asked her.

'She's very happy about it, so is my father, although my sister thinks it's awful. But that's because she's in love with Jack Dunlop and can't wait to marry him. What do you really think, Lilli?'

'You'll make a marvellous nun,' Lilli said. 'But they'll cut all your hair off.'

'I don't mind,' Dorothy said. 'Nobody'll see it.'

I was waiting now for Dorothy to ask Lilli what she

would be doing, but though I could detect the question on the tip of her tongue it stayed there. Whatever subtle understanding these girls had for each other it was enough to stop the question, and I knew that if Dorothy couldn't ask the question I certainly should not.

We went on talking about school subjects, sports and the books we were reading (I had just discovered Dumas, whereas Lilli was reading *Les Miserables* and Dorothy Jeffrey Farnol) until the little French clock chimed six. Then Lilli got up and opened the library door and said to Miss Dalgleish: 'I'm putting the kettle on,' and she left us to make the tea in the kitchen.

'Kit, come in here,' Miss Dalgleish said. 'Dorothy: you help Lilli.'

Dorothy smiled understandingly and said 'All right, Miss Dalgleish,' and I went into the library. It was not a very large room but its walls were solid with books, and in the centre were two tables facing each other. One was a large mahogany library table and the other (Lilli's because it was stacked with her schoolbooks) was a smaller escritoire with little drawers on each side. Near the window was a cabinet gramophone and around it were stacks of records, and along one wall was a large leather couch.

'You like books, don't you?' Miss Dalgleish said as if it were an order rather than a question.

'Yes, I do,' I said.

'Lilli says you read quite a lot.'

'As much as I can.'

'Then I'm sure you respect books and look after them.'

'Of course.'

'In that case you can borrow any two books you like except any from that glass-fronted case over there. And I don't think you'll need encyclopaedias.'

I glanced at the stacks of the *Encyclopaedia Britannica* and a ten volume *Dictionary of Religion and Ethics*.

'Take your time,' Miss Dalgleish said. She had been writing, and though I noticed the black-covered notebook she was using I didn't know then its significance in Lilli's life. She put on her spectacles and went on writing, and I began to browse around the shelves.

They were neatly organised into poetry, plays, biographies, fiction and paperbacks. The paperbacks were the white-jacketed Tauchnitz editions in English which she had imported from Germany, and there were dozens of them—all novels. There was also a section for French and German and Italian novels, and on the other side of them a collection of thick dictionaries. One section was given to Australian literature, and there were stacks of larger books about painting and views of foreign cities. There were two more busts near the window and on the mantelshelf, and a couple of small tables were stacked with inlaid plates, silver boxes and figurines in china or metal. When I looked around this room I knew a little more about Miss Dalgleish and probably a lot more about Lilli.

In fact thinking of Lilli I was far more interested in the contents of the library than I was in my choice of books. I felt so flattered to be allowed into the room that I thought I had better not overdo it so I concentrated on the cheapest and simplest-looking books—the Tauchnitz editions. I chose two novels, one by Upton Sinclair called *Mountain City*, and *Arrowsmith* by Sinclair Lewis.

'The tea is ready,' Lilli said from the salon.

'Let me see what you have chosen,' Miss Dalgleish said.

I showed her the books and she looked at me for a long moment and said, 'What are you going to become, Kit? A lawyer, like your father?'

'No, Miss Dalgleish,' I said.

'What then?'

'I want to work on a newspaper if I can.'

'Are you sure of it?'

'Yes.'

Then she surprised me. 'What do you think Lilli should do when she's finished school?' she asked me quietly and I thought rather nervously.

I needed a moment to organise my reply. 'I don't know,' I said. 'But I suppose she'll go to University.'

'You think so?'

'She can do it, if anybody can,' I said.

'And then what? What would she go to University for?'

'I don't really know,' I admitted.

'You think she should become a teacher?'

'Not Lilli,' I said without thinking.

'Well then?'

I said I didn't know, and I had a strange feeling that Miss Dalgleish was defending herself. Women then had little chance of going into any of the professions except teaching and, with luck, medicine. But Lilli showed no sign of wanting to be a teacher or a doctor.

'You see!' Miss Dalgleish said as if she had been argued with and had won her case, and I wondered if this was one of the strong, silent arguments she was having with Lilli.

'The tea is getting cold,' Lilli called out.

'Yes . . .' Miss Dalgleish got up and I followed her into the salon. 'All right, you can pour it,' she told Lilli who took the cosy from the silver teapot and poured the tea into Miss Dalgleish's fine, white bone china cups.

The sandwiches were thin and the forks for the cakes were silver. The cakes were made by Mrs Peters; delicious; and finally Miss Dalgleish lifted a white cloth from a large, confectioned cake and said, 'Today is Lilli's seventeenth birthday and Mrs Peters baked her a special cake.'

I saw Lilli's head go down.

'Oh no!' Dorothy said. 'That's not fair.'

Lilli looked embarrassed. 'I didn't want you to know.'

'You should have told us,' Dorothy said unhappily.

'Oh, it doesn't matter,' Lilli told her.

'It does matter,' Miss Dalgleish said. 'She wouldn't allow me to tell you before you came, but I insisted that when you were here you should know.'

We wished her many happy returns and Lilli didn't thank us but kept her eyes on her plate.

'She didn't want any fuss,' Miss Dalgleish went on, and again I had the impression she was on the defensive, while by saying nothing at all Lilli seemed to be on the offensive.

I knew that this was another fragment of the subtle, unknowable, endless disagreement going on between them, and I wondered if it had finally reached the problem of Lilli's future. Thinking about it and watching them both I decided that Lilli wanted to go to University and Miss Dalgleish didn't want her to. I was sure of it, and I knew now what Dorothy Malone meant when she said that she had to be loyal to the secret part of Lilli's life. If this was part of the secret I felt as Dorothy did—I was on Lilli's side. It was only when I eventually read Lilli's black book that I discovered it was Miss Dalgleish who wanted Lilli to go to University and Lilli who didn't want to, and I suppose it was logical that even in the matter of her future it was Lilli who decided how much she would accept and how much she would refuse.

'The cake's marvellous,' I said to break our awkward silence.

'I'll tell Mrs Peters. She'll be pleased,' Miss Dalgleish said. 'Lilli fill the pot please and give them another cup.'

Lilli did as she was told, and though I expected her to be resentful with Miss Dalgleish there was no sign of it in Lilli, and that was another puzzle for me. You expected one sort of behaviour from Lilli but often found another.

'I'll give you my present tomorrow,' Dorothy told Lilli.

'No you won't,' Lilli said roughly. 'I don't want anything.'

'It's not fair,' Dorothy said again.

'It's not supposed to be fair,' Lilli said. 'And anyway it's not worth talking about.'

When we had exchanged a few more pleasantries about the town and the latest fire it was time to go.

'Go and get the basket for Kit and the flowers for Dorothy,' Miss Dalgleish told Lilli who went into the kitchen and returned with a basket of fruit and a large bunch of chrysanthemums. Lilli gave me the fruit (we had the same selection in our own garden) and Dorothy the flowers.

'It was very nice of you to come,' Miss Dalgleish said, 'and I hope you will come again.'

We thanked her and, as Tilley began to bark in anticipation of someone leaving, Lilli told Miss Dalgleish that she would take him out. 'I'll walk Dorothy home,' she said.

'All right, but take the key and lock the gate when you go out.'

We left the old fortress, and Lilli locked the gate behind

her as if, for a fleeting moment, the drawbridge had been let down and must now be sealed up again.

'You didn't mind, did you Kit?' Lilli said as we stood for a moment before parting.

'I enjoyed it. Honestly,' I said. 'And I finally saw the statues.'

'Don't say anything about me becoming a nun, will you,' Dorothy said to me.

'Kit never says anything to anybody,' Lilli told her, and I loved Lilli then. That is, I loved her in my own fashion. There was nothing between us but friendship; and statements like that from Lilli confirmed for me what a good friendship it was.

'Goodnight, Kit,' they said.

'Goodnight,' I told them, and I walked home wondering again what Lilli's future would be. It was obviously not going to be easy, but every time I saw Lilli now I knew she was about to bloom. It was obvious that a combination of Miss Dalgleish's disciplines and Lilli's stubborn contention to be herself was on the verge of bringing ripe rewards to both of them.

But I was mistaken, because a few days later the Stubecks returned to St Helen and Lilli's life would never be the same again, as if she couldn't avoid the decisions she would have to make simply because she was still Lilli Stubeck and could never be anyone else.

# 10

IT WAS LILLI'S OLD ENEMY, POLY HOWLAND THE CHEMIST'S SON, who called across the street to her: 'I saw your old lady in Nooah, Lilli, and she's coming here to get you.'

Poly had grown into a plump young man who now served in his father's shop and, though he liked to consider himself a jolly fellow who was popular and worth a greeting from everyone in town, in fact he was someone we pitied more than despised because he had been so spoiled by his parents that he could hardly be anything but the thing he had become—a soft-skinned adolescent who still thought cruelty funny.

'Did you hear me, Lilli?' he called after her as she ignored him.

Poly knew that Lilli had given up her retaliations and yet, as she stopped for a moment to look at him, he panicked, laughed, and hurried into his father's shop. Lilli said nothing. She didn't know whether to believe Poly or not. Several times in the last few years there had been casual reports that the Stubeck family had been seen in neighbouring or distant townships, but they had never been reported as near as Nooah.

So Lilli was not surprised when, at 8 o'clock one night, the bell of the big gate rang and when she opened it she saw her mother and her baby brother—little Jackie. It was dark and she couldn't see them properly but she knew at a glance who they were.

'We want to see Lilli.' It was little Jackie who said it and he was peering at the shadowy girl who had opened the gate for them.

'It's me,' Lilli said.

Lilli says in her black book that she had never blamed her parents for leaving her with Miss Dalgleish and taking money to stay away. She had never felt, given her family life as it was, that there was anything cruel or abnormal in it. It fitted so easily into every other aspect of the Stubeck family behaviour that she had even accepted the fact that they had left her there year after year without question, without thought. So that now, when they had returned, Lilli was dispassionate enough to face them calmly.

'Let us in,' Jackie said boldly.

'Come on then,' Lilli said and pushed the gate open wide. They walked through and Lilli slammed it shut. She now faced a curious choice—to take them to the front door of the house or through the back door to the kitchen. Lilli led them to the back door, and when she held open the wire door for them to enter the well-lit kitchen she received her first shock.

Her memory of her mother was of a very large woman in voluminous clothes, with a thick, brown face, strong arms, an iron grip, a powerful voice and a manner that fitted her bulk. But the woman who walked into Miss Dalgleish's kitchen looked as if her body had been lost somewhere in the torn clothes that had once been big enough for her bulk. Her face, once large and healthy, was now pale and flabby, and her eyes hunted around the room in the old way but with a frightened sort of void in them. She walked with difficulty, and she said to Lilli, 'I'm sick, Lill, and I've got to sit down.'

It was little Jackie who seemed to be in charge. He was now ten years old, and though he was small and thin and his three-fingered hands were curled up in front of him like little claws, he looked wiry and brown. Though big-eyed with obvious hunger, he was wildly alert.

'Hello Lilli,' he said.

'Hello Jackie,' Lilli said, and knowing that she too was being inspected she realised how much astonishment there was on both sides, because what her mother saw was a girl of seventeen on the verge of coming to womanhood who was self-possessed, neatly and expensively dressed, and with not much left (visibly) of the urchin who had closed the gate on Matty and Mrs Stubeck six years before.

'Where's the Missus?' Mrs Stubeck said to Lilli as if she had noticed nothing.

'She'll be here in a minute.'

'Could we have a cup of tea and something to eat?' Mrs Stubeck asked in a begging voice. 'We haven't eaten all day.'

Lilli had been preparing herself to stand up to her mother, but already it was obvious that there was nothing left to stand up to and she knew that the person she had to talk to here was little Jackie.

'What did you come for, Jackie?' she asked.

'To get you, Lilli,' Jackie said.

Lilli was still watching them — but almost from a distance. She had removed herself.

Again her mother said: 'Where's the Missus? I've got to talk to the Missus . . .'

By now Mrs Stubeck and the bare-footed Jackie had established themselves in the kitchen as if they had no intention of ever leaving it. They were sitting at the table watching Lilli who switched on the electric kettle and went out into the hall and called out to Miss Dalgleish: 'It's my mother. She's in the kitchen.'

When Miss Dalgleish came into the kitchen and saw the Stubecks she said, 'What are you doing here, Mrs Stubeck?'

Mrs Stubeck looked at Jackie as if he would have to do all the talking, particularly with Miss Dalgleish.

'We came for Lilli,' Jackie said in a small but commanding voice.

Miss Dalgleish ignored him. 'Well?' she said to Mrs Stubeck.

'We just wanted Lilli,' Mrs Stubeck said. 'And we need some food. We haven't eaten all day.'

'Lilli will give you some food,' Miss Dalgleish said, 'but if Mr Stubeck sent you to get Lilli you can tell him that he can't have Lilli and you can say that is absolutely final.'

Then Lilli, who was cutting bread and meat for them, saw something she had never seen before. Her mother began to cry. She blinked; huge tears appeared, and she began to pick helplessly at her hair. 'Matty isn't with us,' she said. 'That's why we came for Lilli.'

'Where is he then?'

'In Queensland,' Mrs Stubeck said.

'Well Lilli is certainly not going to Queensland with you,' Miss Dalgleish said, and left the kitchen.

Mrs Stubeck turned to Lilli and said, 'You don't know what happened, Lill . . .', and Lilli learned in a few miserable sentences from her mother what the rest of the town discovered later about the family, although my version of it is a combination of Lilli's account and the story little Jackie told me.

The trouble began when Matty was arrested for robbery with violence. After leaving St Helen the family had moved from town to town for almost five years, and eventually they had gone as far north as Townsville in Queensland. There, Matty and Bob, the eldest son, had tried to rob a hotel, not with a gun but quietly through a back window which led to the little office where there was a cash box always sitting on the desk with a few pounds in it.

The aim was a petty theft that would almost have gone unnoticed in the town, but they were surprised by an old man who slept in the next room. When he tried to stop them escaping, using a pickaxe handle as a weapon, Bob had taken the handle from him, and in the struggle that followed the old man had been knocked down. In falling he had bumped his head on the desk and died almost immediately. Hearing the struggle, other members of the hotel family had arrived, and though Bob got away Matty was caught.

Nothing more was heard of Bob who simply disappeared, but Matty was tried as an accessory and given a life sentence, which in those days was generous because the normal punishment for an accessory to murder was hanging.

For the next eighteen months the remnants of the family had roamed all over Queensland and New South Wales, but one by one the others had deserted: first another of the boys, Geordie, then one of the girls married an opal miner, and thereafter in one town or another the other two boys (men now) had simply walked off and after them Alice who had already been living with a broken-down boxer. The remnants of the family had gone off with a sideshow from one of the travelling fairs and then Grace, who became pregnant, lost herself in the city where she could dispose of the baby.

That left Mrs Stubeck with Jackie, and they had worked their way through New South Wales, living more or less as beggars until Mrs Stubeck fell ill. Almost helpless then, they had walked right across New South Wales pulling a handcart and surviving by begging and stealing on their way to the one possible salvation for a chronically sick woman and a ten year old boy with crippled hands—to Lilli who had always been the brightest and ablest member of the family.

# 11

THE FIRST WE SAW OF MRS STUBECK AND JACKIE WAS THEIR reappearance in the old house by The Point. Almost instinctively Mrs Stubeck had gone back there, and for her luck the house was empty. Moreover it was in slightly better condition than usual because Tom Johnson, the last occupant, had been an unemployed itinerant carpenter with two children and, with scraps of wood and old doors and windows taken from other wrecks, he had repaired the facade. He had also used mud from the river to give the kitchen a clean and solid floor. Tom (a Mason) had abandoned it when the local Masonic Lodge had found him a better house and given him enough work to escape the wretchedness of The Point.

So Mrs Stubeck and Jackie moved in, and once more the streets and shops and butter factory and dairies and butchers and bakers and backyards were visited by a scavenging Stubeck — by the lively, three-fingered ten year old Jackie who pulled a handcart which ran on bicycle wheels. When the town learned what had happened to Matty and discovered that Mrs Stubeck was ill there was a certain amount of sympathy for her. We all knew what conditions were like in that old house by the river, and the dirt and neglect of both Mrs Stubeck and Jackie suggested that once more The Point would become a pigsty and a slum.

What we watched with curiosity and a lot of gossip was Lilli's behaviour. What would she do about the family?

Lilli obviously knew what she was doing when she visited The Point, and what she found was the bare and dirty wreck she knew so well, with no furniture and no

Stubeck belongings except a few blankets and some pots and pans which Jackie had carried on his little cart. There was a dirty mattress on one floor where her sick mother spent a lot of her time, and in the kitchen were half a dozen fruit boxes that served as tables and chairs. They had one hurricane lamp and not enough wood for the fire, and whatever food they begged (or that Lilli brought with her) would not last long. Above all, it was obvious that Jackie was the provider of everything they had, and Mrs Stubeck could do little more than boil potatoes and fry onions and poke the fire and complain that Jackie had not brought enough wood to keep it going.

It took Lilli a few days to decide, but one night she moved into The Point with some clothes packed in one of Miss Dalgleish's old leather suitcases, and the next day she walked into every shop on the main street asking for work. For her luck the local photographer, Jim Bailey, had just lost his shopgirl assistant, and Lilli got the job. It was a quick transformation for Lilli, almost as sudden and brutal as the one that had installed her with Miss Dalgleish, and though we were surprised that Miss Dalgleish had allowed it to happen like that, we wondered why Lilli had done it. And, like almost every family in town, we speculated about it.

'I don't see why she had to move to The Point,' my mother said. 'Why couldn't Miss Dalgleish have done something?'

'Done what?' my father said. 'The only thing Miss Dalgleish could do would be to take on the responsibility for Mrs Stubeck and the boy, and if she did that it would be forever, and I can't see Miss Dalgleish burdening herself with three Stubecks.'

'But it's so drastic—what Lilli has done. It's incredible.'

'What else could the girl do?' my father said. 'Somebody has to be there to look after the mother and the boy, and someone has to provide for them.'

'I still feel that Miss Dalgleish could have done something so that Lilli could stay at school.'

'Short of employing someone at The Point to look after Mrs Stubeck, which no one in this town would agree to, what could she have done?'

'Did you talk to her, Kit?' my mother asked me.

'To Lilli?'

'Yes.'

'No. I haven't seen her since she left school.'

'It's all wrong,' my mother insisted.

We all thought it wrong, but what could anyone do about it? Miss Hazel, our head woman teacher, called on Lilli at The Point. She was shocked to see Lilli living in that slum, but Lilli told Miss Hazel that it was her own affair and nobody else's. Since Miss Hazel could not offer any real help or serious alternative, she had to walk away from the situation and try Miss Dalgleish. But Miss Dalgleish would only say that it was Lilli's decision and there was little she (Miss Dalgleish) could or would do about it. Miss Hazel told Dorothy Malone that Miss Dalgleish was obviously very bitter, and reluctant even to talk about it.

'They're both so stubborn,' Dorothy said, 'that you can't help them. And they've really separated, Kit. Over such a thing.'

So once more the town was curious to see what would happen to Lilli. We saw her now in her new role as a shopgirl and photographer's assistant, and (to the cynics) in her old role as a gypsy and a Stubeck. Every morning she walked from The Point down the main street to Jim Bailey's shop where she sold films, took in films for developing and printing, took orders for photographs (weddings and christenings and parties) and in the afternoon went into the darkroom with Jim Bailey (the only man in our town who wore a beard) who began to teach her how to develop and print films. She was paid twenty-five shillings a week, which was a starvation wage for three people.

Lilli kept herself neat and clean, though how she did it at The Point was a mystery, and how long she could go on being neat and clean was something to speculate about. We never saw Mrs Stubeck on the streets. She seemed to have given up whatever it was that had kept her going, as if now that Lilli was in charge there was nothing left for her to do. But Jackie was everywhere, and Lilli didn't discourage him because she needed all the loot that Jackie could bring in: old potatoes, eggs, scraps of meat, chopped wood, spoiled buttermilk, the very things that Lilli herself had once raided the town for.

Inevitably Sergeant Collins called on Lilli one night and wanted to know why a ten year old like Jackie wasn't attending school. Next day Lilli took Jackie to the elementary school, to 'Boom' MacGill who was still teaching, and left him with a pencil and a copy book and an admonition to stay there and not run away. But Jackie was still as wild as a bird, and an hour later he walked out of school and was seen wandering around the back streets of the town. When Lilli took him back the next day he ran away again, and thereafter Lilli didn't try to force him—not until he had been brought before the magistrate's court.

From the outset Lilli was fighting a losing battle because her twenty-five shillings a week might keep them all in some sort of food and a little kerosene for the lamp, but winter was coming on and she still had no beds to sleep on, only one mattress on the floor, two blankets, and no warm clothes for Jackie or Mrs Stubeck. She didn't even have a broom to sweep the floor with, and Jackie was never able to supply enough chopping wood to keep the stove going. Above all it was Mrs Stubeck who was the burden. Although she was able some days to cook a meal and get water from the river, most days she spent in chronic misery hunched before the stove, or lying down on the mattress on the floor.

It may be difficult in our modern society of social welfare and health authorities and rich charities to remember what it was like when there were no social services, no state medical care and (in our town) only a few religious women's organisations that acted as charities but were in fact little more than distributors of old clothes and tins of tomato soup. Though Mrs Stubeck was chronically ill the Stubecks, including Mrs Stubeck herself, had never thought of seeking medical attention. Who would pay for it, and what good would it do? Lilli took her to our cottage hospital which two of our local doctors gave time to every week. Lili worked six days a week and had to take a morning off without pay to accompany her mother; when

Dr Kelly examined Mrs Stubeck he said she had an infected liver and a swollen spleen and gave Lilli a prescription and told Mrs Stubeck to stay in bed.

Some of us watched and admired Lilli's efforts to look after her mother and Jackie, but all attempts by the ladies of the town to sympathise or ask questions received short answers. In fact the first change we noticed in Lilli was this resort to rudeness. If the charitable ladies gave her something she took it, but she was never grateful. So we knew that we were watching a reversion to the old Lilli, because in her years with Miss Dalgleish she had at least become much more tolerant and almost polite.

The real mystery for us was Miss Dalgleish. We still did not know what had happened between Lilli and Miss Dalgleish, except that it was obviously uncompromising. In the six years Lilli had spent with Miss Dalgleish the town had unconsciously come to think of each of them as part of the other, and perhaps it was only when Lilli left that people began to realise how close they had become in their daily lives and in their mutual dependence on each other. There was a lot of talk about how much Lilli owed Miss Dalgleish, and how grateful she should be. But you had to know Miss Dalgleish and Lilli to understand why Lilli could do what she had done, and why Miss Dalgleish seemed to accept it without pity or apparent interest. It was simply a fragment of their stubborn resistance to each other.

But it was sad to see Miss Dalgleish make her journey down the street on Saturday mornings without Lilli beside her. It was 'tragic' to think that they had separated. And yet, as in all family quarrels in a small town like ours, we thought it might be resolved — either by Lilli abandoning her family, or by Miss Dalgleish agreeing to do something for them.

# 12

THEN, ONE SUNDAY MORNING, MISS DALGLEISH WAS SEEN walking down to The Point with Tilley on a lead.

Until now Miss Dalgleish had never been near the house on The Point and she arrived to find Lilli washing clothes in an enamel basin set on a box outside the front door.

'I've brought you Tilley,' she said as Tilley leapt excitedly around Lilli's legs and began barking. 'You should have taken him in the first place.'

Lilli bent down to rub Tilley's nose and respond to his affection. Then she said, 'He can't stay here. I can't look after him.'

'You'll have to,' Miss Dalgleish said. 'I'm going away, and Mrs Peters can't manage him if I'm not there.'

'How long will you be away?' Lilli asked.

'I'm going to Europe,' Miss Dalgleish said, 'so I'll be away at least a year and it would be cruel on the dog to keep him shut up in the house and the garden. So you must take him.'

'All right,' Lilli said.

'Why are you wearing your school uniform?' Miss Dalgleish asked Lilli.

'To save my other clothes,' Lilli said.

'I want to see inside the house,' Miss Dalgleish told her, as the real condition of Lilli and the house and the surroundings became overwhelmingly obvious.

Lilli was aware that Miss Dalgleish was sickened by what she saw, and she knew she was being ordered to expose herself. 'I don't want you to go in there,' she said.

'Why not?'

'Because it's disgusting,' Lilli said.

'In that case I had better see it,' Miss Dalgleish told her, and walked into the house.

By now Jackie had acquired from somewhere in the town a broken armchair, two kitchen chairs and a deal table, but there was still only a mattress on one of the bedroom floors and no other furniture. Lilli's attempt at neatness (food in boxes, clothes hanging on nails) had made little impression on the dirt floor of the kitchen and the stained walls of the two other rooms. Mrs Stubeck was sunk in the old armchair before the stove, and when she saw Miss Dalgleish she got up with difficulty and said:

'Sit down, Missus. Sit down there,' and she pointed to one of the kitchen chairs.

'No thank you, Mrs Stubeck. I'm not coming in.' After a few steps and a glance around the house Miss Dalgleish was already in retreat. 'Are you any better?' she asked Mrs Stubeck from the door.

'I can't get around,' Mrs Stubeck said. 'I've got to leave everything to Lilli.' Then, in a sudden panic: 'You're not going to take her away are you?'

'No. I brought her dog.'

'You can't take her away, Missus,' Mrs Stubeck said miserably, as if Miss Dalgleish's reply made no sense to her. 'You won't do that, will you?'

'That's not why I'm here,' Miss Dalgleish said.

'I can't do without Lilli,' Mrs Stubeck said, in tears.

'I'm not going to take her away,' Miss Dalgleish said irritably and rejoined Lilli who had not followed her into the kitchen. 'It's awful,' she said to Lilli who had not interrupted her washing.

'I told you not to go in there,' Lilli said.

'You are ruining your life,' Miss Dalgleish said. 'Wasting it!'

'Yes,' Lilli said.

'They're not worth it.'

'It doesn't matter,' Lilli said dispassionately, watching Tilley who had been liberated to chase wildly along the river bank after one decadent smell or another. Jackie had also arrived with his little cart laden with firewood stolen from backyards or picked up where it lay around.

'Hello, Miss Dalgleish,' Jackie said as if they were old

friends. Jackie wore a torn pair of short pants whose braces were attached with nails. He wore no shoes and no socks, and his stance was that of a small dog standing up to a big one.

'Go away,' Miss Dalgleish said to him angrily.

It was only when I read Lilli's account of Miss Dalgleish's visit to The Point that I realised how Miss Dalgleish, from the outset, had decided to deal with Jackie and Mrs Stubeck. They simply didn't exist, or ought not to exist, and by removing them totally from her horizon she was removing them from any consideration she or Lilli might owe them. It was something Miss Dalgleish often did to the whole town.

I have to remind myself, reading Lilli's version of it, that Miss Dalgleish was a very rich old lady who had always lived like a rich old lady, and her self-justifications were often as ruthless and simple as Lilli's were complicated and deceptive. On the surface Lilli's behaviour seemed straightforward. She wasn't going to leave the responsibility for her sick mother to a ten year old boy who himself needed attention. But there was obviously more to it than that, because even in this Lilli was still stubbornly defending herself against that total absorption by Miss Dalgleish which she had always resisted at all costs.

When Miss Dalgleish said 'Goodbye, Lilli,' and walked with her tight little steps up the dirt road into the town, Lilli watched her until she was out of sight. Then she walked down to the river and sat on the bank watching the swollen, grey, winter flood race around the curves of what was in summer our swimming hole. She sat there for a long time until Tilley found her. She stroked Tilley gently until he too became impatient and left her. Then she walked back to the house to finish washing the basinful of knickers, stockings and slips, and the tangle of torn and filthy woollen underwear which was her mother's gesture to hygiene.

I suppose that day was the end of something for Lilli, because one can almost trace her steady disintegration from the moment Miss Dalgleish left town. In the weeks and months that followed, and until Miss Dalgleish's

eventual return, Lilli reverted more and more to the old
Lilli who was on her own in the town, neither for it nor
against it, but wary of it and cut off from it. I think the first
thing we noticed was her changing appearance. Her good
clothes couldn't take the strain, particularly in a house
with no electricity, no cupboards, no proper washing
facilities, no lavatory, a very dirty kitchen and a muddy
approach. Lilli could wash her clothes but she couldn't
iron them, and it showed. Her shoes began to look scruffy,
her hair became a little more tangled for lack of proper
washing and care, and a smudge here and stain there on a
skirt or a jumper were inevitable in that house, or even in
the darkroom where she worked in the afternoons.

It was not a question of Lilli giving up. Lilli always
behaved as if her conditions were normal, as if she had
never lived with Miss Dalgleish, so that there was no sign
of self pity or regret or suffering. There was no suggestion
either of Lilli taking on the airs of the genteel poor. On
the contrary she was not ashamed to do what she had
always done as a child—pick up anything that seemed
useful. She was not ashamed to accept gifts, and when she
accepted them she did so without any hint of obligation or
appreciation. I suppose it was this attitude more than any
other that disappointed many people in town who expected
Lilli to suffer nobly and with high principles. But Lilli
took what she could get and didn't say thank you for it. So
once again the town looked on Lilli as a local outcast who
deserved little pity and more contempt. After all she had
been born a gypsy.

And there was Jackie. Twice more he had been taken
forcibly to school by Sergeant Collins, and then Mrs
Stubeck had been summoned to the magistrate's court for
failing to see that he attended school. It was Lilli who
attended the court and said that she would make sure
Jackie went to school and stayed there all day. But a few
weeks later Mrs Stubeck was summoned again and this
time Lilli was warned that, if he persisted in staying away
from school, the next time a summons was issued it would
be because Jackie was in need of care and protection,
which could mean that he would be sent away to an

orphanage in Bendigo where he would be looked after.

'Do you understand, Lilli?' the magistrate, Mr Badewell, said.

'Yes,' Lilli said. 'I understand.'

'He'll be taken away.'

'I know.'

'Do you understand it, Jackie?' Mr Badewell said.

Jackie nodded.

'You'll end up in a home if you don't go to school. You've got to go to school and that's all there is about it. You understand?'

'Yessir,' Jackie said.

I don't know what Lilli's methods were with Jackie. But I do know that she didn't punch or pinch him, like her father, or use her mother's iron grip. I never heard them quarrelling, in fact they always seemed to get on very well. But Lilli must have persuaded him this time, because Jackie stopped playing truant, although it was doubtful if he learned anything at school.

I suppose he was another disappointment for those who wanted Lilli to justify those years with Miss Dalgleish. They wanted her to transform little Jackie from a scavenging urchin into a useful little boy who, though poor, would do his best to be attentive and respectable. But Lilli made no such effort, and Jackie's sins were marked up to her as a failure. Mrs Stubeck didn't count because we thought of her now as little more than a human cabbage.

I suppose I felt as disappointed as everybody else that Lilli hadn't managed to rescue little Jackie from what was obviously going to be a hopeless future. I liked Jackie because I liked Lilli, or rather I liked him because he had the same irrepressible commitment to survival.

Unlike the rest of the Stubecks, Jackie was a good fisherman and in the last days of the summer that was now gone I had shown him where the best fishing holes were and how best to bait hooks and lay his lines. After a few lessons he had become expert enough to equal my catch, and sometimes he would come and sit by me and talk about his adventures en route from Queensland to St

Helen. It was then that he gave me his version of his father's crime and punishment.

Jackie's three-fingered hands didn't bother him. His wrists and thin arms were weak, but his reduced fingers seemed to gain extra agility. He was a nervous boy and you couldn't help looking at them as they folded and twisted and pinched at things. Tilley the dog took him over. Tilley had abandoned Lilli because he was now in his element—companion to a scavenger with a licence to do as he pleased. His coat became dirty and shaggy and his temperament untouchable. He barked when he wanted to bark, and when Jackie was at school and Lilli at work he roamed the town from one end to the other until 4 o'clock when he waited at the school gate for Jackie to appear. In fact Tilley had become a Stubeck, and we were now so accustomed to the Stubeck methods of survival that we accepted the sight of Tilley searching the town as part of their tenuous existence.

But I didn't realise just how tenuous the Stubeck existence had become and how difficult it was for them to survive on Lilli's twenty-five shillings a week until the night Lilli woke me up and asked for help.

I still slept on the verandah even in winter, and it was about midnight on a rather cold night when I was awakened by Lilli pushing me in the ribs.

'Wake up, Kit,' she said. 'Do wake up.' (Lilli still used some of Miss Dalgleish's expressions.)

'What are you doing?' I said, sitting up, startled.

'I'm trying to wake you up, but you sleep like a log.'

'Shhhh . . .' I said. 'What's the matter?'

'Jackie's caught in a trap, and I can't get him out.'

'Where?'

'At the Carroll's place.'

The Carroll house was in a corner of a dead-end street which bordered the racecourse and beyond that open country. It wasn't more than five minutes away, and when I thought of Jackie and the Carroll's place I knew it meant stolen chickens.

'What happened?'

'I told you,' Lilli said impatiently. 'He's caught in a fox

trap and I can't get him out. I need your help, so hurry up.'

My clothes were inside the house. I opened the glass door quietly, pulled my trousers on over my pyjamas, put on my shoes without socks, and joined Lilli who was waiting by the bed.

'Hurry up,' she said. 'He's hurt.'

'All right,' I said. 'Only for heaven's sake be quiet.'

We tiptoed along the verandah and once on the paths Lilli pulled me by the sleeve and began to run, and because ours was a quiet town there was something eerie and exciting about running breathlessly through it in the middle of the night. Lilli took me through the heavy bushes that lined the racecourse and we more or less crawled along a chicken wire fence which bordered the big yard of the Carroll's property.

'Jackie,' Lilli said. 'We're here . . .'

There was a gap in the chicken wire fence, or rather a hole near the ground, obviously a hole opened deliberately so that a fox could easily find it. But instead of a fox finding it, Jackie had. He was half-sitting and half-lying on his side near the hole, and as I bent over him I could see that his left arm was caught in a steel trap which was attached by a chain to one of the fence posts.

'What happened?' I said as I tried to open the trap.

'I put my hand through the hole to crawl under it and there was a trap there.' Jackie was obviously in pain and he had been crying.

'I couldn't open it either,' Lilli said as she watched me struggling with the trap. 'It won't move.' She was calm, almost offhanded, and though I didn't expect anything else from Lilli I knew it was for Jackie's sake.

I had seen this kind of trap before, but I had never used it. It was a clever device for catching foxes. Unlike a rabbit trap, or gin trap, this one was designed to capture a fox by the leg without doing too much damage to the valuable skin, although it slapped shut with great force. It had two flanges which overlapped, and a sort of cylinder which clamped on the fox's leg when he stepped on the flanges. Jackie's arm was caught in the cylinder, and being thicker than a fox's leg it was squashed. When I tried to open the flanges against the spring they wouldn't budge.

'It's got some kind of lock on it,' Lilli said.

I tried to pull the trap's chain from the fence so that I could handle the trap better, but it was well nailed down.

'Don't make a noise,' Lilli said as one of the Carroll dogs began to bark.

I knew that the secret of the trap must be in some kind of locking device that kept the cylinder shut. It was too dark to see it properly so I bent down close to it and felt all around the cylinder with my fingers until I found a little clip that fell into place, automatically locking the cylinder. I lifted it and then tried to push down the flanges, but the spring was heavy and I couldn't do it.

'Hurry up,' Lilli ordered. 'Those dogs are barking, and he's going to faint.'

'No, I'm not,' Jackie said, but I knew he was near it. He was a frail little boy, despite his wiry appearance.

'You open the cylinder when I stand on the flanges,' I said to Lilli. Standing up I started to put all my weight on the flat pieces of steel which released the spring, and as it began to open I said to Lilli: 'Now release the catch on the cylinder and watch your fingers.'

'Go on,' Lilli said and shouted at Jackie: 'Pull your arm out.'

Jackie pulled his arm out and I told Lilli to let the cylinder go. I lifted my foot and the spring shut with a steely, frightening snap.

'Let's see your arm,' I said to Jackie.

Even in the dark I could tell that it was badly cut and squashed, and by now it was covered in blood. Jackie was holding his injured arm with the other hand and moaning.

'You ought to take him to hospital,' I said.

'No, you don't,' Jackie said. 'I'm all right.'

'Listen, Kit,' Lilli whispered as the dogs barked again. 'Can you set the trap and cover it up the way it was?'

'I think so.'

'Well do it and put it back. I don't want the Carrolls to know it was set off.'

'Why not?'

'They'll know it was Jackie,' Lilli said.

'You'll have to help me,' I told her.

It was not easy, and Lilli almost lost her fingers twice when the flanges snapped shut before she could pin them down with their little catches. But when I had done it I put the trap under the fence, covered it with sand, and cleaned up all signs of our presence. Then, with the Carroll dogs barking furiously enough to wake up anyone who was expecting a fox, we ran along the fence and through the bushes and up the empty road.

Jackie was now very weak and we had to help him.

'You'll have to do something with his arm,' I said.

'All right. But let's get him home first.'

We half-ran, half-walked through the street and down the dirt road to the river, with Jackie holding tight to my arm on one side and Lilli holding him on the other side. When we arrived at The Point Lilli opened the kitchen door and Tilley rushed out, barking and jumping on Jackie until Lilli slapped him and told him to be quiet. Then she lit the oil lamp and sat Jackie down on one of the kitchen chairs.

'Put your arm on the table and I'll fix it,' she said.

By the light of the oil lamp we had our first view of Jackie's wounds, and though they looked messy I could see that they had not penetrated too deep.

'Can you move your fingers and your wrists?' I asked him.

Jackie was keeping his mouth firmly shut but he wriggled his hand and his fingers which meant nothing was broken. I waited for Lilli to boil some water to cleanse the wounds but the Stubecks had their own remedies. Lilli cut an onion in two, and using one half of it as a swab she cleaned the arm carefully, ignoring the real tears that were running down Jackie's dirty face.

'I'll get some rags,' she said.

She went into another room (I could hear Mrs Stubeck snoring in there) and returned with a paper bag which had clean strips of cloth in it, and it was only years later that I guessed what those rags were really for. She took the second half of the onion and cut it into flat rings and spread them on a cloth and wrapped it around Jackie's arm, tying it very tight.

Lilli hadn't commiserated with Jackie, or said a soft word of sympathy to him, and Jackie accepted it all without question or complaint. 'Go and lie down,' she said to him.

Jackie did as he was told and I noticed then that there were also tears in Lilli's eyes. But I knew they were onion tears, although Lilli was embarrassed by them and turned away from me to wipe them away with her fingers.

'What was he after?' I asked her.

'Never you mind, Kit,' Lilli said as if it were better for me that I didn't know.

'All right. All right. But you must have been crazy.'

'They shouldn't be allowed to set traps in town,' Lilli said.

'But they were after a fox.'

'What sort of a fox?' Lilli said bitterly.

In fact it wasn't difficult to work out what had happened. Jackie had obviously raided the Carroll's henhouse before and, blaming a fox rather than a Stubeck, Andy Carroll had planted his trap to catch it. What surprised me was Lilli's attendance, and it was then that I realised how barren their food stocks must be to get Lilli into a night-time raid on a chicken coop with Jackie as the thief.

'You won't say anything, will you?' Lilli said to me.

'You know I won't.'

'If they find out what Jackie was up to they'll send him away to that place in Bendigo. They're just waiting to catch him.'

I knew she was right. 'Who am I going to tell?' I said to her.

'You've got blood on your pyjamas,' she said, 'and your mother will want to know where it came from.'

'Damn!' I said, wondering how I would explain it.

'Tell her your nose was bleeding,' Lilli said.

I laughed. 'I'd never have thought of that,' I said, and at that moment I heard Jackie crying quietly in the next room. 'You ought to get Jackie to the hospital,' I said again.

'In the morning,' she said. 'If I go at this hour they'll get suspicious.'

'What'll you tell them?'

'That he was setting a rabbit trap.'

'Haven't you got some aspirin or something for him?'

'No. It's the onion that's stinging now, but he'll feel better in a little while. Good night, Kit,' she said, dismissing me.

'Good night, Lilli,' I said.

She didn't thank me for my help and I didn't expect her to, but I went home that night with a new kind of admiration for Lilli because, like almost everybody else in town, I had been taking for granted what Lilli was doing. In a curious way we were all too sure of Lilli, accepting without question that she would do what she had taken on. I suppose it was a backhanded compliment that we thought of her like that but as a result we hadn't bothered to notice how difficult it was for Lilli to keep Jackie and her mother alive.

If she had been a little more helpless and grateful the town might have been more charitable and concerned. But Lilli was too self-contained and self-sustaining to attract concern. In fact she didn't want it; that was the point, but I went to sleep that night wondering how long she could keep it up.

# 13

AROUND ABOUT THIS TIME THERE ARRIVED IN OUR TOWN A MAN who would eventually play a significant role in Lilli's life, although at first it was no more than a casual relationship which began on the street corner outside Lilli's photographer's shop.

His name was Abraham Devlin, and even his name told us something about him. 'Devlin' was Irish and New Testament, but 'Abraham' was an Old Testament name which suggested a parent who had some angry biblical thunder in him. I always imagined that something opposite had turned Dev into a gentle, sometimes helpless, innocent man who nonetheless had his own powerful convictions.

Devlin had come to St Helen as the reporter on our local paper, *The Sentinel*, a job I would eventually have myself. He didn't strike me as a real newspaperman, although since then I know how varied the breed can be. Instead, he was something of a freak. His arms were too long for his sleeves, his trousers were a little too short, and his manner was often so abstracted that some days he saw you and was friendly and remembered everything about you, whereas other days he didn't see you at all and seemed almost to forget exactly who you were, although he was always gently and carefully polite and never mean.

It didn't take long for the local larrikins to realise that they had a perfect victim in Dev, and they teased him about his hair, his dusty shoes (a little too big for him) and his distant, childlike, blue-eyed stare. This was only a beginning. Devlin acquired an old bicycle which seemed as odd as the man himself, and my own memory of him and his bike is the sight of him forever pumping up its tyres which the boys or the larrikins in the town were always letting down.

'Why do they do it, Kit?' he said to me one day when he had been visiting my father's office and, in the space of a few minutes, had found his tyres flat.

'God knows,' I said.

'Up to the age of ten I understand it,' he said. 'After that it's very odd.'

'They're just teasing you,' I said.

'It must be more satisfying than that,' he said, and then he did something which only Devlin would do. There was another bicycle leaning against a verandah post which belonged to Ron Hardy, the manager of the record shop. Dev walked over to the bicycle and let the air out of the back tyre, then out of the front tyre, and he stood back for a moment as if expecting some sort of revelation from it.

'What on earth did you do that for?' I asked him.

'I wanted to see how it felt.'

In the meantime Ron Hardy, hearing the hiss of air from his tyres, ran out of his shop, and finding Dev standing over his bicycle and the tyres flat said: 'What the hell do you think you're doing, Dev?'

'It's all right, Ron,' Dev said. 'I'll pump them up again.' And he turned to me and shook his head. 'You see,' he said. 'It means nothing at all.'

'It depends on the man,' I suggested.

But that was something Dev didn't understand. He never understood wickedness in others. Yet he was a good reporter, and he always seemed to choose the smallest and most significant incidents to report the biggest and most significant events. I remember his story about the biggest herd of sheep the town had seen for years. He didn't mention the herd itself but concentrated on a lost lamb that wandered through the town bleating and looking for the rest of the sheep until he was chased by half the town and finally herded with the others into the sheep yards, there to wait for death. It was very well written and was a sad and amusing little story.

His one idiosyncrasy — the one that gave Devlin his real reputation in our town — was his politics. Although politics is hardly the word. 'Philosophy' perhaps. Even 'religion'. It was certainly a faith with Dev. In any case, from a surprising man it surprised us, and it revealed itself one Saturday night.

Saturday was the day when the farmers of the district came to town, and the shops in the brightly-lit main street stayed open until 9 o'clock. Almost everybody was in town to parade up and down, see friends, eat in the restaurant and, if they had travelled more than twenty miles (and the regulars who lived in town had always 'travelled' more than twenty miles) drink in the pubs. It was therefore a crowded, cheerful town that collected on our main street under the sloping verandahs. There was no real amusement except the cinema, so the parade and the shops and the Salvation Army band were our entertainment on the streets.

The point I should make is that as a town we were dependent on the big and small wheat and wool farmers on both sides of the river, as well as the dairy farmers along the Riverain, the citrus growers to the south, and the vini-culturalists to the north. The town survived by servicing them, so our town population was almost entirely non-productive. We had no real working-class except about ten people at the butter factory, twenty on the railways, and another twenty on the council and stockyards and telephone and electric system. Our society had little political or ideological inspiration in it.

So it was startling one Saturday night for the crowds in the street to see Devlin put a little wooden box on the pavement not far from the biggest pub and right outside the photographer's shop where Lilli worked and begin to speak: the first time anyone had done such a thing. If Devlin had simply started to speak from the footpath we would have said he was round the bend. But because he brought a box and was standing on it we identified him easily as a soapbox orator.

It is hard to say what sort of an audience Dev expected to collect in our country town, but it is even more difficult to imagine anyone in that street listening to what he had to say because what Dev talked about was Utopia. Like almost everybody else in the town I would eventually listen to Dev, but it was only when my father gave me the clue to understanding what he was saying that I realised how serious he was, and that Devlin's real reason for that soapbox was an attempt to educate us in the history of Utopian thought.

'He thinks he's another Sir Thomas More,' my father said, and since the only thing I knew about Sir Thomas More was that Henry the Eighth had cut off his head I asked a few questions. My father told me that More took the word Utopia from the Greek which simply means 'no place'. 'Which was his name for some tropical island with a perfect society that ran itself, with everything shared and nothing owned. The trouble with More's ideas is that he knew what an ideal state should be,' my father said, 'but he didn't say how we were going to achieve it.'

With his gentle, passionate conviction Devlin told us that our society could become perfect if it wanted to be, and that Sir Thomas More had given us the simple ideas we should strive for: all labour and its product to be shared, sex equality, a six-hour day for everybody, equal education for all, no exploitation of any kind, all dress to be uniform, and all medicine and social services free for all.

On that first Saturday night it took only a few minutes for the barracking to begin. After ten minutes Dev's 'meeting' had become hilarious entertainment for a fair-sized crowd who, grasping at one or two words from his text, teased him with witty repartee about sex equality, and appointed Devlin the future dictator of St Helen. 'Hail Dev!' they kept shouting. They also had a lot of fun with the idea that we would all have to dress alike—like Dev himself.

By the time I was on the street that night Dev had finished his talk and had gone home, but I heard about it en route and I dropped in on Lilli at the shop to ask her what had happened.

'Nothing happened,' she said. 'Devlin got up and began to talk and everybody laughed at him.'

'He must have known they would,' I said.

'It didn't seem to make any difference,' Lilli said.

'Why? What did he say?'

'I don't know,' Lilli replied reluctantly. 'Something about Sir Thomas More.'

That was all I could get out of her.

Devlin came back every Saturday night thereafter and we were soon used to seeing him there on his box talking to the naked air. Most of the novelty wore off, though someone would heckle him at least once a night, or some of the boys from the pub would make a raid on him, pull him off his box and mimic his style, he became a sort of weekly fixture like the Salvation Army band. No matter what they did to him he never retaliated, he never fought back.

In time, and to the very end, Devlin would take us week by week through the whole history of all the Utopian movements, from Campanella's *City of the Sun* to the Moravian Anabaptist communities, to the Levellers, the Diggers, Coleridge and Southey's schemes at Oxford, German Pietists, Rappites, the Perfectionists, the Shakers, Ephrata, the Manana Society, the Oneida Community, Robert Owen, William Morris, the Hutterites in South Dakota, Everhard Arnold's modern Bruderhof movement and finally the Sermon on the Mount.

I suppose the only person who was a permanent audience or heard all his theories and his dissertations almost to the end was Lilli, who could hear it all from inside the shop and later from Devlin himself. Being a good reporter, though comparatively new in town, Devlin knew Lilli's story, and every Saturday night after his dissertation he would stop and talk to her. I should say he 'tried' to talk to her. Lilli was no more co-operative with Dev than she was with the rest of us, but at least she tolerated him. Probably because he was the victim of so much mockery and larrikin fun, although his refusal to resist or retaliate must have annoyed her.

I don't know what they said to each other, although whatever was said I am sure it was Dev who did all the talking, while Lilli would listen impassively and non-committally and offhandedly as she always did. Dev could hardly avoid talking to her about his perfect Utopia, but he was also a good conversationalist on plenty of other subjects because of his simple curiosity in everything, and Lilli was always a good, if impenetrable listener. Jackie liked him, and once or twice we saw Devlin dinking Jackie home on his bike after school.

Having established their friendship thus far, it has to be left there because there was as yet no significance in it. What Lilli was really going through at the time (apart from the problems of poverty) was a worsening in her mother's condition and the possibility that she would lose the house on The Point.

We were eating supper one night when there was a knock at the back door and my mother sent my sister Jean to see who it was. Jean came back saying, 'It's for you, Kit. It's Lilli Stubeck.'

'Lilli?'

'Yes, Lilli.'

I went to the back door and Lilli didn't bother with any preliminaries. 'Does your family have a doctor, Kit?'

'Well, we usually go to Dr Dixon,' I said.

'Would you come with me to see him?'

'What for?'

'My mother's very bad and she needs a doctor.'

'You don't need me,' I told her. 'Why don't you go down to Dr Dixon yourself?'

'Because he won't come if I ask him.'

'How do you know he won't?'

'Because I already asked Dorothy's doctor, Dr Foran, and he said to take my mother to the cottage hospital. And how am I supposed to do that?'

'All right,' I said.

When I told my mother what I was doing she came out and asked Lilli if there was anything she could do. 'Do you want me to go back home with you, Lilli?'

'No thank you Mrs Quayle. I just need a doctor.'

'Do you want to phone him?'

'No, that's no good.'

'Then Kit will go with you,' my mother said.

I wasn't at all sure how effective I could be, but because

Lilli had some faith in it I hurried along the street with her the few blocks to Dr Dixon's house. Lilli didn't talk, and I knew better than to say anything.

At the gate she hesitated a moment. 'Do you think he'll ask me for money right now?' she said.

'I don't know,' I said. 'He doesn't usually. He sends a bill.'

'That's to you.'

'Let's try him anyway,' I said.

Dr Dixon was a comparatively young doctor with a red-haired wife and an open Chrysler car. He lived in one of the newest houses in town and it had an electric bell which I pushed. Mrs Dixon came to the door. She looked curiously from Lilli to me. 'Hello, Kit,' she said. 'What's up?'

'Can we see Dr Dixon?' I asked her.

'He's just finishing his tea, but I'll get him.'

She didn't invite us in and we waited on the top step until Dr Dixon came out with a napkin still in his hand.

'All right, Kit. What do you want?'

'This is Lilli Stubeck,' I told him, wondering how best to do this.

'I can see that,' he said. 'So?'

'Her mother's ill and she wants you to take a look at her.'

'Where?'

'At The Point.'

'What's the matter with her, Lilli?' he asked.

'She keeps fainting, and I can't always wake her up.'

'Who's been looking after her?'

'Me.'

'I mean medically. She's been ill for some time, hasn't she?'

'Yes.'

'Then who attended her before?'

'I took her to the cottage hospital.'

'Can't you get her there now?'

Lilli shook her head. 'She can't move. She can't walk.'

'Did you try to get the ambulance?'

Our ambulance service, like our fire service, was organised by volunteers. 'They won't send it unless a doctor has seen her.'

Dr Dixon sighed. 'And what are you here for Kit?' he asked me.

'Lilli didn't think you would come if she asked you herself,' I said.

'And you think you make the difference?'

'I don't know, Dr Dixon,' I said. 'Dr Foran's already refused to go down there.'

'Oh has he? And what makes you think I'll go?'

I didn't say anything, and as Lilli and I stood there silently I could feel Lilli preparing to turn away and leave. But I didn't move.

'Oh, all right,' Dr Dixon said. 'Get in the car and wait for me. I haven't finished my tea yet.'

We waited in Dr Dixon's Chrysler for ten minutes until he came out with his black bag. He got in, started the car and drove down to The Point without saying a word, although he was whistling gently and glancing at me in the front seat from time to time. I felt more and more like a copy of Lilli who was sitting silently in the back seat.

It was already dark, and when Dr Dixon walked into the kitchen at The Point and saw the oil lamp he said, 'Haven't you got electric light down here?'

'No,' Lilli said, telling Tilley to stop barking.

'Have you got another lamp?'

'No.'

'All right. Bring that one,' he told Lilli and though I was standing in the doorway I could see that Mrs Stubeck was now on a bed—an old wire mattress, which was obviously another of Jackie's acquisitions, raised off the floor on boxes.

Jackie, his arm still bandaged, had been sitting in the kitchen putting an axe handle into an axe head when we arrived and he joined me outside when the light disappeared.

'What do you think's wrong with her, Kit?' he asked me as if I was now some sort of oracle, since I had brought the Doctor.

'I don't know, Jackie,' I said. 'Nothing much probably.'

'She keeps talking to herself,' he said. 'She's never done that before.'

'She'll be all right,' I told him.

'She can't even stand up.'

Jackie had seen his mother through a lot of trouble, and until Lilli had taken over he had been his own counsellor. But now he was looking for reassurance in his childish way and though I wasn't the best person to give it to him, I was all that he had at the moment.

'She'll be all right,' was the best I could do.

'You think so, Kit?'

'Of course.'

'She keeps crying.'

'She's sick.'

'Maybe it's something Lilli gave her to eat.'

'Yes, it could be that.'

Jackie went on like that until Dr Dixon came out, and as he threw his bag into the car he asked Lilli if he could wash his hands.

'I'll do it,' Jackie said and he took an enamel basin that was leaning against the wall, filled it with water from an old oil drum near the door, and put it on a box. Lilli brought some soap from the kitchen and a grey-looking towel, and we waited for him to say something.

'She'll have to go to hospital,' he said. 'I can't do anything for her here.'

'Can you tell the ambulance to come?' Lilli asked him.

'Yes. But get her cleaned up. She's filthy.'

'You mean wash her?'

'Yes I do. Is this the way you live, Lilli?'

'Yes.'

'My God,' he said. 'I can't believe it in this day and age in a town like ours. And you knew about this, Kit?'

'Yes.'

'Did Miss Dalgleish ever see this place?' he asked Lilli.

Lilli refused to answer.

'What did she say about it?'

Again Lilli refused to answer, and Dr Dixon was about to pursue it when I quickly interrupted him, knowing that Lilli would probably turn rude if he asked any more questions about Miss Dalgleish. It was none of his business.

'Can I ride with you up the hill?' I asked him.

'All right, get in,' he said and he told Lilli that he would arrange for the ambulance to be there as soon as possible. 'Though heaven knows when that'll be. I'll try to find the Jackson brothers. Maybe tonight, maybe tomorrow morning. But have her ready, Lilli. Put a clean dress on her. Has she got one?'

'Yes.'

'All right. I'll see her in hospital,' he said. He looked at Jackie for a moment, shook his head, and got into the car. I was already in it, and when we reached the main street he stopped to let me out. He asked me if anybody from the town ever went down to The Point.

'Nobody that I know,' I said. 'Only Sergeant Collins, and Miss Hazel, one of our teachers. But I don't think anybody else has been down there.'

'It's incredible,' he said. 'How does the girl manage?'

I knew how she managed but I wasn't going to go into it with Dr Dixon. 'She hasn't got any money to pay you, Dr Dixon,' I said, hoping thus to persuade him not to ask for any.

'Never mind that,' he said. He drummed his fingers on the steering wheel. 'Something ought to be done about that place,' he said.

I thought he meant it as a need to improve it or help Lilli and I wanted to warn him about Lilli's lack of gratitude and her curious way of taking help without question though rarely asking for it. But I decided against it. It was never any use trying to explain Lilli to other people, and Dr Dixon must have noticed that she hadn't thanked him for coming to The Point. It was something of a turmoil in my mind, so I was surprised and bothered when I discovered what he really meant.

'That place ought to be condemned,' he said, half to himself.

I sat up. 'You can't do that,' I said. 'It's the only home they've got.'

'Nonetheless I ought to do something about it, Kit. It's been a filthy slum for twenty years and it ought to be pulled down.'

'But not while Lilli's there,' I said.

'Oh, they can find something else,' he said. 'It's no place

for that girl and her mother and that boy to live.'

'Where else could they go?' I said.

'I don't know, but they shouldn't be there at all,' Dr Dixon insisted as he put the Chrysler in gear. 'Nobody should be forced to live in a place like that.'

I knew that Dr Dixon was influential enough as a doctor to get some kind of public health ruling on The Point, and I also knew that he was doing what he thought best without understanding Lilli's real condition. Nobody really knew much about Lilli. Yet I didn't say anything to Lilli about it. I didn't want to add to her problems, and I suppose I hoped that Dr Dixon wouldn't do anything about it. After all, plenty of other people had complained about The Point and its itinerants before, but nobody had ever done anything about it.

But this time I was wrong, and my father would do what I hadn't done—he would tell Lilli that somebody was complaining about The Point and that there was a good chance that it would be pulled down, and he would tell her at our dinner table.

When my mother heard that Mrs Stubeck had been taken off to hospital she told me that I should invite Lilli to eat a hot lunch with us on Sunday. She would prepare it on Sunday rather than Saturday if Lilli would come.

'You'll have to ask Jackie, too,' I pointed out.

'Then ask him.'

'He's only got three fingers on his hands,' I reminded her, not knowing myself how Jackie manipulated his knife and fork, and always ready with warnings about Stubeck behaviour.

'But surely he can manage,' my mother said.

'I suppose he can,' I said. 'In fact he's pretty clever with his hands.'

'Then tell them to come on Sunday.'

Lilli was unpredictable in a situation like this. A free meal was welcome but it would have to fit in with her particular rules of behaviour at the moment, and I wasn't sure what they were these days. I left school one lunchtime and went down to the photographer's shop and found her making up the accounts. She now ran the shop by herself.

She had become a very good developer and printer of films so that Jim Bailey was usually out of it, looking for more photographic work in the district. I asked her about her mother and she said she was being looked after, which was all that she would say.

'Well my mother wants you and Jackie to come and have dinner at our place on Sunday,' I told her.

Lilli looked hard at me as if trying to measure something — although what she was looking for I didn't know. 'What for?' she said.

'No reason. She told me to ask you, that's all.'

Lilli hadn't taken her eyes off me and I knew enough to keep my eyes fixed firmly on hers. 'All right,' she said. 'I'll come.'

'With Jackie,' I told her.

'Yes.'

I didn't look forward to Lilli's visit any more than I had years before when she had come alone. I hoped she wouldn't come. But when Sunday morning came she turned up at the back door and asked me if she was on time.

'We haven't got a clock,' she said.

She was exactly on time and I noticed that she wore her good tweed skirt and her Fair Isle jumper, both of which looked as if they had been tightly folded for some time. Jackie was the surprise. He wore a scruffy pair of black shoes without socks, and his shirt and short pants though worn and crushed were clean and almost respectable. I wondered what clothes line they had come from.

'Hello, Kit,' Jackie said. 'Did you see my arm?'

He pulled back his sleeve and the bandages were off. Blood had hardened on the open wounds and there were long bruises up to his elbows, but it looked healthy and I asked why he had taken the bandages off.

'Lilli says it's better like this,' he said.

I think we all got through that meal with memories of Lilli's last visit. What we watched for this time was not so much Lilli's behaviour as Jackie's. My mother had given us all clean napkins, including one for Jackie, and when he picked it up and unfolded it and put it on his lap we knew that Lilli had told him what to expect and what to do. He also knew that he had to wait while my father said grace; he knew that he was not supposed to eat until we were all served. And, in slyly watching him manipulate a knife and fork with his three fingers, we hardly noticed Lilli who ate her meal with a curious restraint, a prim sort of discipline which was like a faint echo of Miss Dalgleish.

But Jackie, despite his little graces, reminded me of the old Lilli. He gobbled his food hungrily and was careless though not inept with his fork, so that peas fell on the tablecloth and gravy was spilled on his trousers. My excuse for Jackie, or rather for Lilli, was that she had to stick to essentials with Jackie. There were enough pressures on him without Lilli insisting on the proper use of knife and fork in that dirt-floored kitchen at The Point.

The real difficulty was conversation, and I suppose we simply talked around Lilli and Jackie, although we did try to include them when we could. My mother tried again to find out more about Mrs Stubeck, but Lilli would only tell her that they were giving her liver to eat and some sort of injections.

'She doesn't faint any more,' she said.

My father then asked her if she knew anything about the nephews of Mrs Carson. Mrs Carson was the old woman who owned The Point.

'No, I don't know anything about them, Mr Quayle,' Lilli said.

'Do you have any contact with anyone of the family?'

'No,' Lilli said.

'Did Mr Landsdown the Town Clerk call on you?'

'No. I haven't seen him.'

'Well he called on me, Lilli, because I once helped old Mrs Carson in a civil suit. The old lady's been dead for years, and Mr Landsdown says that the Shire Council is trying to find out who owns your house at The Point now.'

'Nobody owns it,' Lilli said. 'It's been abandoned for years.'

'That's true, but somebody owns it,' my father said. 'In fact, the local authorities have decided that they want to demolish it. That's why they are trying to find out who owns it.'

It took a moment for Lilli to realise what my father was telling her. 'Demolish it?' she said incredulously. 'What do they want to do that for?'

'They didn't tell you anything?' my father said.

'No.'

'Somebody's complained about the conditions you live in down there.'

'Who?'

'I don't really know . . .' My father knew who it was but didn't want to involve Dr Dixon with Lilli.

'It was Dr Dixon,' I put in. 'He told me he was going to do it.'

'It's none of his business,' Lilli said. 'We've always lived at The Point and nobody's ever complained before.'

'There's always been talk of pulling it down,' my father said gently. 'But I suspect it was your mother's illness that decided Dr Dixon to do something about it.'

Lilli didn't say where will we go? She didn't protest. But I knew what she was thinking, I knew that cat's-eye look. If the town demolished The Point she would, if she could, demolish half the town in retaliation. I hadn't seen that sort of threat on Lilli's face for a long time.

'Surely they can't just pull it down and leave Lilli and her family homeless,' my mother said.

'If they get a court order they can do what they like,' my father told her.

'Isn't there some way of stopping them?' I asked him.

'You might stop them pulling it down, or delay them. But they could probably get an intermediate order condemning it for habitation.'

'When will they do that?' Lilli asked him.

'I don't know, Lilli. It's just talk at the moment.'

'Couldn't you stop them condemning it?' my brother Tom said, because we were all in this now, and though I was the only one in the family to have seen inside that slum, we were defending it to a man.

'The only way to stop them condemning it is to prove that it is perfectly habitable,' my father said.

Lilli knew and I knew that The Point was not habitable at all, but she didn't ask for my father's help. We finished the meal with rice pudding, and as if another old friendship had been revived Lilli found Mickey's head on her lap. Our Mickey was now an ageing little dog. He had been asleep by the fire, but some distant memory must have stirred him, and Lilli played with his nose and his ears and said 'Hello Mickey. You didn't forget me.' It was softly said and I remembered the ten year old Lilli who had whispered in his ear before. Mickey licked her hand in response.

We were now waiting for my father to put his napkin into its ring and when he did so Lilli put hers on the table and Jackie did the same.

'I'll see what I can do, Lilli,' my father told her. 'But I can't promise very much, you understand.'

'I understand,' Lilli said. She didn't thank him, but unsmiling as always she did thank my mother who gave her a paper bag with eggs, butter, tea and sugar and some old clothes of Tom's for Jackie. When we were outside she pulled my sleeve and said to me angrily: 'Why didn't you tell me Dr Dixon was going to ask the Council to condemn The Point?'

'I didn't take it very seriously,' I told her.

'What do you think your father can do?'

'You should have asked him,' I said.

'Goodbye, Kit,' she said to me.

Jackie had already gone, and it was one of Lilli's real achievements that Jackie left us without taking anything with him.

# 14

ABOUT A WEEK LATER MY FATHER TOLD US AT DINNER THAT he had found a judgment in one of the appeal court records that made it 'unallowable' for a local authority to demolish a building without the owner's consent unless it was a danger to life and limb, or a threat to other buildings, or put public health at risk. He said he had pointed this out to the Town Clerk, and that Mr Landsdown had come up with a surprising piece of news.

'Miss Dalgleish now owns The Point,' my father said. 'They were looking for the Carsons and they checked the Land Registry office in Melbourne and discovered that Miss Dalgleish bought the property from one of the Carson boys a month ago.'

'But she wasn't even here,' I said.

'She probably did it through her Melbourne lawyers rather than Strapp, her local lawyer. In any case there is no more talk for the moment of pulling the place down.'

'But what on earth does she want with that old slum?' my mother asked.

'Hard to say,' my father replied. 'But it's obviously got something to do with Lilli.'

'Did you tell Lilli?' I asked him.

'Yes.'

'What did she say?'

'She didn't know what to say at first. She's never been very communicative, that girl, but I think this time she was genuinely speechless. Then she asked me what the old lady wanted it for. Why would she buy it?'

'That's what I'd like to know,' my mother said again.

'That's not all,' my father went on. 'Miss Dalgleish is on her way home.'

'Already?'

It was six months since Miss Dalgleish had sailed for Europe, and because she had made it known in the town that she would be away for at least a year we thought something must have happened to change her mind.

'That's also something to do with Lilli,' my mother said.

So we waited, intrigued, for Miss Dalgleish's return, and it was a period of curious respite for Lilli. With her mother in hospital she had one less mouth to feed, and there was no more talk of condemning The Point because Miss Dalgleish obviously had plans for the place if she had bought it. But what sort of plans? Was she going to take pity on the Stubecks and clean the place up for them? Or was she so disgusted with it that she wanted to force Lilli out? We were back once more to that old puzzle of their tense and fragile relationship, but to me it seemed no more than a continuation of whatever it was that had always bound Miss Dalgleish and Lilli together, or had divided them so cruelly. It was still there, and we watched Mrs Peters now to see if she might unwittingly give us some clues.

In Miss Dalgleish's absence Mrs Peters had maintained the big house, and it was known from the postman, Mr Edwards, that Miss Dalgleish had written to her from France, Italy, Austria and England. We also knew that Mrs Peters had called regularly on Lilli at the photographer's shop and had told her what was in those letters. And, as if there was something inescapable in the intense and preoccupying relationship of those three women behind their high wooden walls, Lilli sometimes gave Mrs Peters her dresses and blouses to iron, rather than to Dorothy Malone who had offered to do them for Lilli.

'It's odd,' Dorothy said to me, 'but I think Lilli still really lives in that house. It's where she belongs.'

Nonetheless Lilli was very conscientious about her mother. One of the nurses, Miss Singleton, told my mother that during Lilli's visits Mrs Stubeck spent most of the time weeping and begging Lilli not to desert her and Jackie.

'She doesn't know her own daughter,' I said when my mother was telling us what Miss Singleton had said. 'Lilli would never desert them.'

'Perhaps not,' my mother said, 'but the poor woman can't help remembering that everybody else did.'

'Not Lilli,' I said.

It was about now that Devlin began to play some sort of a role in Lilli's life and, looking back on it, I can't help feeling that Lilli may have allowed it to happen in anticipation of Miss Dalgleish's return. It was almost a counter-relationship in advance, a counter-balance in advance, a defence in advance. I think my guess was borne out not only by what I knew of that relationship but by subsequent events.

In any case Devlin was now seen cycling down to The Point in the evenings, and he was sometimes seen cycling home from The Point in darkness. Maybe Jackie's presence spared them any real scandal, or perhaps it was too much to imagine that Devlin would do anything wicked, or that Lilli would allow him to. Nonetheless there was gossip, and when I asked Dorothy Malone what she knew about it Dorothy herself was puzzled.

'They're so odd,' she said. 'I was there last Sunday when Dev came, and the first thing he did was to strip down to his bathing trunks and step into the river.'

'But it's winter and the river is still in full spate,' I said. 'It must have been freezing.'

'That's what I said to Lilli, but she didn't seem to think it odd. She told me Dev couldn't swim so she had to keep an eye on him in case the current swept him away.'

Even expert swimmers didn't venture into our river in winter because it was too dangerous as well as being too cold.

'When I told him he must be crazy and asked him why he did it,' Dorothy went on, 'he said that every time you plunge into natural water you are reborn. It helped re-create the autonomic nervous system.'

'What did Lilli say to that?' I asked.

'Nothing. In fact anything Dev did or said seemed perfectly normal to Lilli and hardly worth noticing. You know, Kit, they seemed to know each other very well, not by what they said but in the way they accepted each other. He sat with us in that awful kitchen drinking Lilli's tea and listening to everything Lilli and I said to each other without saying a word. And Lilli ignored him. Then he took a little book from his pocket, it was covered with newspaper, and said: "Now I'll read you girls something from William Morris's *News From Nowhere*", and without waiting for either of us to say anything he read us a whole chapter of it. Have you ever heard of it?'

'Yes.' In fact I had heard of it from Devlin himself during one of his soapbox dissertations.

'It's all about a trip up the Thames.'

'No, it isn't,' I said. 'It's about the English going back to handicrafts and nature to find perfection after a revolution.'

'Who told you that?' she said.

I had to admit that it was my father who had told me. In fact he had said: 'It's William Morris's version of More's *Utopia* and Campanella's *City of the Sun*.'

'I was bored,' Dorothy said, 'but Lilli didn't seem to mind. She just sat there and listened, and when he had finished she said to him, "I think it's time for you to go." And Dev said, "All right, Lilli," and just rode off.'

I laughed.

'What are you laughing at?' Dorothy asked me.

'It's exactly the way I would have pictured them together,' I said. 'Don't you think it's funny?'

'I didn't think it funny as much as odd,' Dorothy said.

'Well aren't they both rather odd?' I said.

'I suppose you're right. The curious thing is that Lilli gave up reading when she left Miss Dalgleish, as if that was all over for her. But I think she liked being read to.'

'Maybe that's what Dev does every time he visits her,' I said.

Dorothy thought for a moment and said, 'Perhaps you're right. But I wonder what Miss Dalgleish will say when she hears about them. She won't like it a bit.'

# 15

MISS DALGLEISH RETURNED ONE LATE SPRING DAY ON THE TRAIN from Melbourne. Mr Malone's Marmon was waiting for her at the station as the train pulled in at 5 o'clock. Almost nobody saw her because she walked straight to the car and waited for Mr Malone to bring her hand luggage. But somebody did notice that one of her arms seemed stiff and that she used a walking-stick and limped slightly. At her age it seemed possible that she had had a stroke, even though she hadn't mentioned it in her letters to Mrs Peters.

We didn't see Miss Dalgleish on the street, not even on her usual Saturday morning visit to the shops. Mrs Peters came and went, and for a while nothing happened. Then one Friday night when I came home from school my mother said that Miss Dalgleish had telephoned.

'She wants you to go and see her tomorrow morning at 10 o'clock,' my mother said.

'What about?' I asked.

'She didn't say.'

'Why does she always ask you if I can go there instead of asking me direct?' I said.

'I think she considers it a courtesy to me. In any case I said you'd be glad to go.'

I groaned. I didn't want to lose a whole Saturday morning visiting Miss Dalgleish. Yet I didn't really object because I was curious, and that Saturday I rang the bell and Mrs Peters opened the big gate for me.

'Hello, Mrs Peters,' I said.

'Hello, Kit,' she said and as we walked up the path to the front door she told me that Dorothy Malone was also expected. 'But after you have gone, not at the same time.'

It was so unusual for Mrs Peters to give out any information that I took it as a warning that I was supposed to go before Dorothy arrived.

Miss Dalgleish was waiting for me in the salon. She greeted me, told me to sit down, asked after my mother and father, and then talked about school.

'A few more months and it's all over for you, isn't it?' she said.

'That's right,' I replied. 'It's our final year.'

Miss Dalgleish closed her eyes almost painfully, and I took that as some sort of requiem for Lilli's lost schooldays, although I may have been wrong. In fact I was inspecting Miss Dalgleish, and even with an adolescent's primitive eye I could see that she had aged in her absence. She was still prim, neat and in command, but there was also a hint of a slump, a sagging of something which, for the first time, made me aware that even Miss Dalgleish could deteriorate.

'I want to talk to you about Lilli,' she said, but she didn't go on because Mrs Peters brought in a tray of tea and scones and she waited until Mrs Peters had poured the tea and left the room.

'Do you see Lilli often?' Miss Dalgleish asked me.

'Fairly often,' I said. 'I mean—in passing.'

'Do you visit her at The Point, Kit?'

'Sometimes, but not very often. I chop their wood sometimes.'

'Did you know that I had bought that old house?'

'Everybody knows,' I said.

'Eat your scone,' she said.

I knew that Miss Dalgleish was having difficulty so I ate the scone and waited.

'Tell me, Kit,' she said. 'Is Lilli going back to her old ways?'

'What do you mean?' I asked, bristling a little.

'Don't be upset,' she said. 'I'm trying to understand what has happened in my absence.'

By one means or another Miss Dalgleish seemed to have found out, as always, what the Stubecks had been doing, although I was fairly sure that Mrs Peters hadn't told her much. But she knew.

'Lilli doesn't earn enough to keep all three of them,' I said, 'so she had to get help where she can.'

'That's not what I'm asking you,' she said firmly. 'I want to know if Lilli has been out at night scavenging the back streets.'

To answer that question I would have to make up my mind what I thought about Miss Dalgleish: whether she had Lilli's interests at heart or her own. I had on the chair beside me the two books that I had once borrowed from her and I longed to put them on the table, say a polite goodbye, and get out of this conversation. By now I was considering my visit a mistake. Seeing my hesitation, Miss Dalgleish puckered up her mouth a little and studied my face.

'I'm not asking for your secrets, Kit,' she said. 'I simply want to know the truth, that's all.'

'What do you want to know about Lilli for?' I asked.

'That's between Lilli and me,' she said.

'But you're asking me, Miss Dalgleish,' I said, surprised that I had had the wit to make the point.

'I want to know how much Lilli has regressed,' she said, 'and I think you are the one person who might be able to tell me.'

'Lilli is Lilli,' I said evasively.

Miss Dalgleish tapped her walking-stick on the floor to give emphasis to her reply. 'That's not an answer, Kit. You must not be evasive.'

I knew that somehow I had to remain loyal to Lilli and yet not upset Miss Dalgleish, because a peculiar thing was happening to me. I was beginning to feel sorry for Miss Dalgleish, which astounded me when I realised it. Of all the people in our town Miss Dalgleish was the one person you never imagined to be in need of any kind of pity. I decided then that honesty was the best policy.

'I don't want to say anything against Lilli, Miss Dalgleish,' I said. 'She's had a hard time.'

'You must remember that it was her own choice, Kit,' Miss Dalgleish said stiffly.

I thought she was going to elaborate but she didn't, so I asked her what she was going to do with that old house on The Point.

'That depends,' Miss Dalgleish said. She too was being evasive. 'I suppose it's even filthier than it was when I saw it.'

'No,' I said. 'They improved it quite a bit.'

'How?'

'Oh, they got some old tables and chairs and a bed for Mrs Stubeck, and Lilli keeps it clean.'

'Then you might as well tell me where they got the tables and chairs from.'

'Jackie got them,' I said unthinkingly.

'I thought so,' Miss Dalgleish said. 'They've been scavenging.'

'But what else could they do?' I said. 'They didn't have anything at all. Absolutely nothing.'

But Miss Dalgleish didn't want to hear about their miserable condition. 'She hasn't given up her friends, has she?' she said.

'No.'

'And you have invited her to your house, haven't you?'

'Yes.'

'Did she behave properly, Kit?'

'Of course she did,' I said.

'Do you know Mr Devlin?'

'Yes . . .'

'What does he talk about on the street corner?'

'Utopia.'

'Does Lilli see him often?'

'I don't know, Miss Dalgleish.' I wanted to go now, so I put the books on the table and said, 'I brought back the books I borrowed on Lilli's birthday. I'm sorry for keeping them so long, but thanks very much for loaning them to me.'

'Do you want to borrow more?'

'No thank you, Miss Dalgleish,' I said.

By now there was a little wall of hostility between us, I suppose it was a wall of Lilli; and I think Miss Dalgleish knew that I was not going to tell her much. Or perhaps my answers and my attitude told her what she wanted to know. She didn't ask me any more questions but she seemed reluctant to let me go, and we talked for awhile about books. She told me not to waste time on people like Arnold Bennett or H. G. Wells, but to read Willa Cather and Edith Wharton and German authors like Thomas Mann and Lion Feuchtwanger.

'If you want to write you must try not to think like the English,' she said. 'They are too parochial.'

When I got up to go Miss Dalgleish also got up and walked me to the front door, limping. 'Come and see me again, Kit,' she said, 'and though you probably have no time for reading at the moment, with your studies, you can borrow from my library any time you wish. You should read as much as you can.'

'Thanks very much, Miss Dalgleish,' I said and let myself out through the big gate, wondering what she was going to ask Dorothy Malone; and wondering too what Dorothy would tell her.

Dorothy and I now became the tenuous links between Miss Dalgleish and Lilli, and Lilli wanted to know immediately what Miss Dalgleish had said to me. She woke me up that Saturday night on my verandah, and nothing reminded me so much of the old Lilli as the nocturnal visit and that nudge in my ribs.

'I want to talk to you,' she said.

'In the middle of the night?'

'It's only 11 o'clock,' she said. She had Tilley with her and he leapt on the bed and put his cold nose in my ear. 'I spoke with Dorothy today,' she said, 'and she told me that you had seen Miss Dalgleish.'

'That's right,' I said. 'She sent for me this morning.'

'What did she want, Kit?'

I sat up and for the first time realised what a scandal it would be if someone caught Lilli sitting on the foot of my bed with me in it. It worried me for a moment, although I knew it didn't bother Lilli. It didn't occur to her.

'She wanted to know about you,' I said.

'Know what?'

Now I wanted to be loyal to Miss Dalgleish, or rather I

didn't want to say anything that would put her in a bad light with Lilli. 'Nothing much,' I said. 'Just how you were.'

'That's not what she asked you,' Lilli told me.

'In effect it was.'

'Yes, but what did she really want to know?'

'All right,' I thought, 'if they are both so desperate to know about each other I might as well tell them.' I shrugged and said: 'Miss Dalgleish wanted to know if you'd gone back to scavenging the back streets at night.'

'What did you say? Did you tell her anything?'

'Nothing. I said you'd been having a hard time, that's all.'

Even in the dark I could see Lilli's eyes open wide. 'What did you say that for?' she said.

'Well . . . she was obviously worried about you.'

Lilli ignored that and asked me if she had said anything about The Point. 'Did she say why she bought it?'

'No. She was pretty evasive about that.'

'Didn't you ask her?'

'Of course I did, but she wouldn't say.'

'Did she ask about my mother?'

'No, but I'm pretty sure she knows all about her. Mrs Peters must have told her. Or maybe Dr Dixon. Or somebody. She always knows what's going on.'

'Is that all she talked about?' Lilli said, getting off the bed and holding Tilley by the collar.

For a moment I thought it best to leave everything well alone, but I changed my mind and decided that Lilli might as well know it all. 'She asked me about Devlin.'

'She did?'

'Yes.'

'What about him?'

'What he talked about on the street corner. That's the way she put it.'

'What did you tell her?'

'I said he talked about Utopia.'

Lilli waited a moment as if there might be more. But there wasn't. She got off the bed. 'Is that all she wanted to know? Is that really all?'

'Absolutely,' I said.

'All right. Goodbye, Kit,' she said.

'What did she say to Dorothy?' I asked her in a loud whisper as she left.

'Nothing,' Lilli answered. 'Nothing at all.'

In other words it was none of my business. But I made it my business when I saw Dorothy on the Monday. We sought each other out because we both wanted to know what had happened. I gave Dorothy a full account of everything Miss Dalgleish had said, and then she told me that Miss Dalgleish had been mainly concerned about Lilli's appearance and about Jackie.

'She asked me if Lilli was keeping herself clean, and if she bathed, and what she did about her clothes. Then she asked if Jackie was hard to manage and if Lilli ever quarrelled with her mother. She asked me what they ate and if Lilli ever borrowed money, or if Mrs Stubeck had gone begging before she went to hospital. I think she was looking for something, Kit, but I couldn't quite put my finger on what it was.'

'Neither could I, but she seems to have something in mind,' I said.

'Between the two of them I wonder if we will ever know,' Dorothy said.

What we both realised was that Lilli had not asked either of us about Miss Dalgleish. Not a word. Like me, Dorothy noticed that Miss Dalgleish was a little lame and used a stick, but she had not mentioned it to Lilli any more than I had.

'It's something you don't think about with Miss Dalgleish,' Dorothy said, '—that something might be wrong with her. And it's something you don't mention to Lilli either.'

I knew that the real answer Lilli wanted would come from Mrs Peters. It would not be Dorothy or me whom Lilli asked about Miss Dalgleish, but the third person in that house. And again I had the feeling that there was a certain continuity in everything that was happening between them, and that their contest in self-possession had simply been taken up where it had left off.

# 16

THE FIRST INDICATION LILLI HAD OF MISS DALGLEISH'S INTENtions was the arrival one Monday morning of the men to put up the electric light poles. Four poles were erected leading from the main power lines to The Point. By the end of the week the line itself was attached and The Point had electricity, including the meter which would tell Lilli how much she would have to pay. This was all done by the local electricity authority, but the wiring of the house had to be done by a private firm, and without consulting Lilli (the doors at The Point were never locked) the Stark brothers wired every room for electric light and put a power point in the kitchen.

The following week Mr Parson the carpenter arrived with a truck-load of posts and timber and again without consulting Lilli he spent the week laying a floor in the kitchen and covering it with linoleum supplied by the Co-op store. Kitchen chairs, a table and a cupboard arrived unannounced, then two beds, a chest of drawers, an armchair, a selection of pots, pans, cups, saucers, plates, knives and forks, blankets, sheets, towels and a washstand with a mirror. Almost every day for a week Lilli would arrive at The Point after work and find Jackie enjoying some new surprise which Lilli accepted as she always accepted cold-blooded manna from heaven.

While this was going on Mrs Stubeck was taken home to The Point by Dr Dixon in his car, and one Thursday evening when I went down to The Point to chop wood and see what was going on I found Mrs Stubeck sitting in the new armchair in front of the kitchen stove. She took no notice of me when I went into the kitchen to get the axe, although I said 'Good evening, Mrs Stubeck. How are you today?' When Jackie arrived with Tilley and a big pail of buttermilk from the factory she ignored him and went on absent-mindedly fingering the yellow brooch which Lilli had returned to her and which was pinned to her dress at the throat. She whimpered to herself from time to time, and what had always been that curious silence of the Stubeck women had become a helpless and vacant stare.

'Are you all right, Mrs Stubeck?' I said to her.

She didn't reply but went on whimpering and fiddling helplessly with her brooch. She was now very thin, but she looked clean and her dress was new and even fitted her. Her shoes were also new, and I guessed that if the clothes were new Miss Dalgleish had provided them. Anybody else in town would have given Mrs Stubeck worn clothes.

Then, one Sunday morning, Miss Dalgleish was driven down to The Point by Mr Malone in the Marmon, and according to Mrs Johnston, who could see The Point from her house near the railway line, Miss Dalgleish stayed there for half an hour. When she left she took Tilley with her.

Nobody in our town could have known what was said that day between Lilli and Miss Dalgleish, and the only reason I know about it is that there is just enough in Lilli's black book for me to reconstruct the conversation. But first of all it is necessary to understand Miss Dalgleish's behaviour in the light of something that Lilli herself didn't know at the time.

Quite simply, Miss Dalgleish had cut short her stay in Europe because she knew that she was dying.

Not only was Lilli kept in ignorance of her condition, but Miss Dalgleish told no one in town except old Dr Wallace, her physician, who would keep her secret. But it became an influence on everything Miss Dalgleish did after her return, although as far as Lilli was concerned anything that Miss Dalgleish did had its own motives and was nothing to do with the fact that she only had a short time to live. Lilli just didn't know. So her responses have to be taken for what they were, a continuation of the usual, complex problems of their relationship.

What Miss Dalgleish said to Lilli that Sunday was simple enough. 'I want you to come back home, Lilli,' she said. 'I will make this house fit for your mother and your brother to live in, and I will pay for their food and their keep. If they need someone to help them I will pay for that too, if you can find someone, but I don't want you living here any more. You are to come home with me and, if you can still do it this year, go back to school; or if not this year then next year so that you can finish your studies.'

Even though Lilli gives me some clues in her black book she is never specific enough to reveal what she said in reply. In general she would never argue with Miss Dalgleish unless it was an issue that was vital to her. As a rule she never reduced herself to details with Miss Dalgleish. But in her own way Lilli's resistance to anything she didn't want to do was brief and stubborn, and she told Miss Dalgleish that she wouldn't go with her.

Miss Dalgleish persisted. 'You can find someone to help your mother,' she said, 'and your brother seems very able to look after himself. I know that you have been scavenging, Lilli,' she went on, 'and that's quite disgusting and you know it. You haven't enough money, I'm sure of that, and you can't really manage, can you? So you would be much better off at home where you can live properly.'

'I'm all right here,' Lilli said, and she told Miss Dalgleish that nothing had changed, and that she was not going back.

Miss Dalgleish then tried to talk to Mrs Stubeck, but though Mrs Stubeck would half-listen and say in a sort of mumbling misery 'Yes Missus' from time to time, she would look up helplessly at Lilli and say, 'You're not going to leave us are you, Lilli?'

'No,' Lilli said each time.

'That's not the point, Mrs Stubeck,' Miss Dalgleish insisted. 'I'm not asking Lilli to desert you.'

'Yes Missus,' Mrs Stubeck said, and by now there were tears rolling down her cheeks.

When she realised that it was hopeless, Miss Dalgleish finally turned to Lilli and said angrily, 'This has gone far enough. It's ridiculous.'

'There is nothing you can do about it,' Lilli told her.

'You will change your mind,' Miss Dalgleish said. 'In the meantime I want to take Tilley with me, so where is he?'

'What do you want Tilley for?' Lilli demanded.

'The neighbour, Mrs Andrews, has cats, and Mrs Peters can't keep them out so Tilley will do it.'

'He won't stay,' Lilli said.

'I shall persuade him to,' Miss Dalgleish replied.

'He's become Jackie's dog now,' Lilli told her.

'Then I'll get him another one,' Miss Dalgleish said.

Lilli did not resist or make any claim on Tilley, not even for Jackie's sake, and she got an old rope they used for Tilley and tied it to his collar. Jackie was outside talking to Mr Malone about the Marmon, and when Miss Dalgleish appeared with Tilley on a lead he said to her: 'Where are you taking him?'

'I'll send you another dog,' Miss Dalgleish said. 'I need Tilley.'

'But he's Lilli's,' Jackie said.

'Lilli is letting me have him,' Miss Dalgleish said. 'He's used to the house.'

'For how long?' Jackie said boldly.

Miss Dalgleish didn't reply but gave the rope to Mr Malone who put Tilley in the front seat, and it has to be said that Tilley went willingly as if anything that happened to him was an adventure he should enjoy rather than resist. He was now a grimy little dog and his coat was matted and wild, but he bounced around on the front seat of the Marmon like an excited child on his way to a party.

Miss Dalgleish's last question to Lilli was about Devlin. Why did he come to see her at The Point? Was it necessary? Wasn't he a silly man?

'There's nothing wrong with Devlin,' Lilli told Miss Dalgleish.

'You're a foolish girl,' was Miss Dalgleish's last remark as she got into the Marmon and drove off. And because Mr Malone was not as tight-lipped as Mrs Peters he told Dorothy that the old lady seemed as always to be in total command of herself, but when he opened the big gate for her he was sure she had been weeping.

I suppose you could almost call the next act an operatic forza del destino as far as Lilli was concerned because a week later Mrs Peters told Miss Dalgleish that in a month's time she would be leaving St Helen for good. She was moving to Nooah, which was thirty miles away. Her years of housekeeping for Miss Dalgleish would have to end.

We all knew the reasons. Mr Peters, who was a mechanic at the Malone's garage, had been offered the garage at Nooah, and though he was no longer a young man he had decided to put all his savings plus money borrowed from the bank into the venture, if not for himself then for one of his sons who was also a mechanic. It meant living over the garage in Nooah and cutting all connections with St Helen, at least for Mrs Peters. She could not stay behind. She could not neglect her husband and son.

That little enclave of Miss Dalgleish and Mrs Peters had been so tight that one always assumed it would go on for ever. And once again there was a lot of speculation about Miss Dalgleish's future now that Mrs Peters was leaving her.

'She'll never find another Mrs Peters in this town,' my mother told my father at dinner when we heard about it.

'Why on earth shouldn't she?' my father said.

'I don't know,' my mother replied, 'but she won't. Mrs Peters never breathed a word of anything that went on in that household. She was as tight as a drum.'

'Oh there must be some woman in town who knows how to keep quiet,' my father said.

'Not the way Mrs Peters did, and not the way she worked. She was perfect for Miss Dalgleish.'

'She'll find somebody,' my father insisted and they left it there because we simply didn't know anything more.

Miss Dalgleish had a month in which to find somebody, and there were several women in the town who would have liked the job. Mrs Smythe, a widow with an unmarried daughter, was the obvious choice. She was clean and motherly and not a gossiper. But she was a bustler, and Miss Dalgleish couldn't stand bustlers. Then there was Aimee Lonstreet, a spinster who had been a helper-companion to old Mrs Rowntree who had lived to the age of ninety-three in one of the three houses she owned. But Aimee was a tall, gangly sort of woman with whispy hair and a rather forgotten look about her, as if she had lost her own personality in the service of others. It was difficult to imagine Aimee successfully sharing the big house with Miss Dalgleish. There were one or two others, but one kind of failing or another made it obvious that they wouldn't measure up to what Miss Dalgleish wanted.

The weeks passed and Miss Dalgleish seemed to have given up looking for anyone; in fact she had now become a recluse. Her failure to appear on Saturday mornings in the town meant that she was rarely seen by anyone. Lilli went on working at the photographer's shop and Mrs Peters still arrived at the big house at 8 o'clock in the morning and left at 4.30 in the aternoon.

Came the final day, however, when Mrs Peters was no longer there, and it seemed as if Miss Dalgleish was going to be left alone. But that same morning Lilli was seen to open the big wooden gate at 8 o'clock and stay in the old house until noon when she went back to The Point. She returned to Miss Dalgleish's at 1 o'clock and stayed there until 5 o'clock when she returned to The Point for the night. She returned the next day and the next, and we knew then that Lilli had become Miss Dalgleish's new housekeeper. Unseen and unknown to anyone but themselves they had come to terms.

I would hear something of what the terms were from Dorothy, and even a little from Lilli herself, but it was really the subsequent situation that made it fairly clear. They had made a businesslike arrangement. Miss Dalgleish agreed to pay Lilli three pounds a week (more than double her present wage) and not insist any more that Lilli abandon The Point. Lilli, for her part, agreed to do all that Mrs Peters had done, but at the same time she insisted on having all the time she needed to look after her mother so she returned to The Point every noon, and every night to sleep.

So the twain had finally met, in the only way they were able to meet: Miss Dalgleish had paid a price for Lilli because the price was right. And Lilli had accepted it because it meant she was better off. At least that was the way it looked. But Lilli, unknowingly, was now attending two women who were slowly dying and who needed her because she had always been a defier of everything, maybe even of death.

# 17

became limp and she was peace off. Or her? This was the way it looked and Lilli was feeling. She was attracting two couples who were simply aloof and who wanted her to establish a way, or a wife's way of everything, and a way of the life.

THEIR DAILY ROUTINE AT THE BIG HOUSE NOW BECAME A CONTEST between Miss Dalgleish's attempt to restore the old relationship, and Lilli's determination to live by the rules of her new situation. Lilli had always had her duties in the house, but the real cleaning and cooking and washing and ironing had been done by Mrs Peters.

'We'll send our sheets and pillowslips to the Chinese Laundry,' Miss Dalgleish told Lilli when they began to establish the way they were going to live.

In their agreement they had decided on the barest essentials of wages and work because they were incapable of sitting down to discuss the details. So their life now would have to be organised in fragments, and Miss Dalgleish began by being the organiser who would shape things her way.

Lilli resisted. 'We don't need the laundry,' she said. 'I'll wash the sheets and pillowslips the way Mrs Peters did.'

'But you could be doing something else,' Miss Dalgleish told her.

'What else?'

'I want you to study, particularly your French.'

'That's over and done with,' Lilli said.

Because Miss Dalgleish never bothered to hear what she didn't want to hear, she refused to acknowledge an argument if she didn't want to argue. 'You'll have plenty of time to study,' she went on. 'You needn't do everything that Mrs Peters did. We'll get a cook.'

'I'll do the cooking,' Lilli insisted. 'That's what we agreed.'

'I didn't agree that you should waste yourself,' Miss Dalgleish said.

Lilli turned away without replying, and thereafter she did the washing and cooking without help from anybody. But because she refused to study, Miss Dalgleish insisted that she spend two hours every afternoon reading to her aloud, which Lilli accepted the same way that she accepted new shoes and stockings and a new dress. But otherwise she was punctilious. She arrived punctually and left punctually. In fact she worked a twelve hour day six days a week because she also had to look after her mother. She dressed her mother every morning before leaving, made her breakfast (and Jackie's), stacked the fire, washed the dishes, made the beds and left everything ready for lunch, which she then returned to give to her mother, who spent the day sitting helpless and half asleep in the armchair before the kitchen fire, even in summer. Sometimes Mrs Stubeck wept when Lilli left her, fearing that she might be abandoned, but she never complained of her health or her loneliness.

I rarely saw Lilli during this period because Miss Dalgleish made sure that The Point had a supply of chopped wood, so there was no need for me to go down there. I did see her occasionally on a Saturday morning when she was shopping alone for Miss Dalgleish and herself. Her rude health was always lovely to see, and now she seemed organised and almost relaxed, as if she was finally doing what she wanted to do. She no longer looked as if she had slipped back to her old ways. She was neat and clean and ironed and washed. Her hair shone and, like her eating habits, her walk had taken on a curious copy of Miss Dalgleish's decisive and authoritative little steps.

But while Lilli bloomed Miss Dalgleish was visibly fading. When she finally emerged one Saturday morning with Lilli she still walked erect but she had to use her stick and she walked very slowly. But she was still in command. It was Lilli who was walking with her, not she with Lilli. They rarely spoke now, and Dorothy (who was almost the only person in town, apart from Dr Wallace, to visit the old house) told me that they behaved like prisoners. 'They can't separate themselves, Kit,' she said, 'and almost everything between them is done without either one of them saying a word. Even when they do talk they seem to leave everything out. Yet you can't really separate them. They're glued to each other.'

I suppose Lilli's life might have gone on like that indefinitely if she had not fallen ill. Lilli was the kind of girl that nature had intended a healthy girl to be, but because she was careless with her body (it was the only thing she was ever relaxed with) the one sickness that would lay her low had to be a serious one, even though it began with little more than a scratch.

On the river bank near The Point there was always a strand or two of loose barbed wire tangled into the mud, and one night when Lilli was filling the kitchen tank with buckets of water carried up from the river, she walked into a coil of rusty wire which the falling level of the river had exposed. Lilli was grateful that she had taken off her stockings, but the barbed wire made a severe gash in her left leg. From her childhood she had been used to frequent cuts and bruises, and as soon as she had stopped any flow of blood she usually ignored them. This time, having washed her leg in the river and stopped the flow of blood she forgot about the gash, except that she wore black stockings to hide it. She worked as usual for the next few days but her leg began to swell, and though she went on working and even persuaded Miss Dalgleish that it was nothing, by the weekend she was unable to walk on it. On the Sunday she was running a high fever, and sometime in the middle of the night she became delirious. At 2 o'clock in the morning Jackie was nudging me awake on the verandah.

'Something's wrong with Lilli,' he said. 'She's talking in her sleep and I can't wake her up.'

I thought of waking my mother or my sister but I was too cautious to take a decision like that where Lilli was involved. At the time I knew nothing about her leg so I wasn't sure whether Jackie was exaggerating what might have a perfectly normal explanation. Nonetheless I pulled my trousers on over my pyjamas, put on my shoes without socks and hurried down to The Point through the purply dark streets.

'Did you wake your mother?' I asked Jackie.

'What for?' he said. 'She can't do anything.'

Jackie took me into the second bedroom which he shared with Lilli. It was no longer bare but had two beds, a mat on the floor, a chest of drawers and a wardrobe. When I turned on the electric light Jackie said: 'Lilli doesn't let us use that.'

'I don't care about that,' I said and took a cautious look at Lilli in bed. She was half covered, and because she slept in nothing but her knickers her breasts were exposed. I had never seen a young woman's breasts before and I blushed and stared and was overwhelmed, but I hurriedly covered her as she threshed her head and shoulders from side to side while her body seemed to leap and jerk in fierce spasms. I started talking to her but she didn't hear me because she was muttering and clenching her teeth and groaning. Her eyes were shut tight.

'It's her leg,' Jackie said. 'It's swollen.'

I was not going to pull down the covers to inspect Lilli's leg but Jackie did. Or rather he lifted the blankets from the bottom and I could see that Lilli's bandaged left leg was bloated and purple from ankle to knee.

'Good God,' I said. 'How long has it been like that?'

'A couple of days,' Jackie said. 'It got worse yesterday.'

It was pointless asking if she had seen a doctor or gone to the hospital, but I knew that she needed a doctor urgently and I would have to get one. I think it was the shock of seeing Lilli in full delirium that gave me the courage to run all the way up the hill to the main street to Dr Dixon's house. It was now almost 3 a.m. and I had to ring the bell again and again before Mrs Dixon came to the door saying: 'Who is it, for heavens sake?'

'It's Kit Quayle, Mrs Dixon,' I said.

'What is it, Kit? Is your mother ill?'

'No, Mrs Dixon. It's Lilli Stubeck.'

'Oh no . . . not the Stubecks again. It's 3 o'clock in the morning.'

'She's very bad,' I said. 'She needs a doctor.'

Mrs Dixon opened the door a crack and asked me what was wrong with Lilli. I told her what I had seen and she said, 'Wait here, Kit,' and a few minutes later Dr Dixon opened the door, pulling on a dressing gown and calling me a 'bloody nuisance'. He asked me to describe the symptoms and was I sure she was serious?

'Tell me exactly,' he said.

Again I described Lilli's delirium, the spasms and her bloated leg and Dr Dixon said: 'That stinking place. I knew it should have been condemned.' But he told me to wait, and in five minutes he reappeared with two bags, one of which he gave me to hold telling me to be damned quiet as we got into his Chrysler. 'Don't slam the door,' he said 'It starts the dogs barking.'

Dr Dixon wanted to know how I had become involved at this hour of the night, and I told him about Jackie waking me up on the verandah.

'Last week that little devil tried to sell my wife a bag of horse manure for the garden, which he had probably stolen in the middle of night from Mr Stuart's stables. And if they're handling manure down there, Kit, this girl could easily have tetanus and that's goodnight.'

'I don't think she would have handled it, Dr Dixon,' I said.

'How do you know?'

'That's Jackie's business, not Lilli's,' I told him.

'I hope you're right, for her sake. It sounds as if it's septicaemia of some sort.'

I have never forgotten that drive through our town in the middle of the night awakening the occasional dog and lighting up a frightened cat crossing the empty road. I suddenly felt rather frightened in our dark, secure streets because I was sure that Lilli was going to die. I had not thought of tetanus until the doctor had mentioned it, but in those days in a country town like ours tetanus was something we feared as much as drowning in our swollen river, or being bitten by a tiger snake. It was always sudden death.

When we arrived at The Point Dr Dixon seemed to accept the fact that Mrs Stubeck had been left asleep and that Jackie was in charge. He told Jackie and me to wait in the kitchen but five minutes later he came out of Lilli's room and questioned Jackie about the gashes in Lilli's leg.

When Jackie told him about the barbed wire the doctor looked at Jackie's dirty three-fingered hands, turning them over and shaking his head.

'Did she handle any of that horse manure you were hawking around?' he asked Jackie.

'She didn't know anything about it,' Jackie said aggressively.

'Are you sure, Jackie, because that could cause tetanus?'

'I didn't even tell her,' Jackie said. 'She didn't even see it.'

'All right, then. I'm going to need your help, Kit,' he said, and he told Jackie to get the fire going and boil some water . . . 'in a reasonably clean pot.'

I suppose the rest of that night must have been a fairly normal example of what a Victorian country doctor in a farming and accident-prone community often had to contend with before there were antibiotics, but to me it was a revelation in how soft and rotten the body could become, and how vulnerable and thin the life force was. Lilli was transformed for me that night from a tough little girl, a self-sustained and unconquerable equal of my age into something captive and destructible. Something outside Lilli's control had finally brought her down.

I had to hold Lilli's arms and naked shoulders while Dr Dixon plunged a scalpel into the swollen leg, and though Lilli was delirious she screamed with pain because the doctor used no anaesthetic.

'Too risky,' Dr Dixon had said when he told me to hold her tight and to sit on the good leg while he plunged the scalpel into the other. I was too much the observer even then to be sentimental, but in Lilli's groans and writhings and delirious jabberings I finally had a complete picture of the girl I knew and yet didn't know. She was simply an eighteen year old girl who was very ill, lying there half-naked with my knees lightly on her legs ('Use your weight,' Dr Dixon had said. 'Just make sure she doesn't move'). Her face was quite defenceless, her guard was down and her secret self-possession was gone. Yet I knew that, even helpless, Lilli was full of life, not death, and I decided then that she wasn't going to die.

Dr Dixon's second bag was filled with cottonwool and

bandages, and now he was soaking up puss and sterilising and staunching the wound. It went on for a very long time, and finally he made a huge pad and bandaged it to her leg and I held it up for him.

'Chuck all that stuff in the stove and burn it,' he said to Jackie. The floor was littered with the soiled cotton wool. 'And then wash your hands.'

'Will she be all right?' Jackie said, and he looked frightened and childish because Lilli's cries had brought him into the room and he had seen the worst of it. 'You're not going to cut off her leg are you?'

'I hope not, Jackie,' Dr Dixon said and he turned to me. 'But she can't stay here. She'll need a lot of constant attention.'

'Can you tell Miss Dalgleish?' I said.

'Not at this hour of the morning.'

'No, but as soon as you can.'

'All right. But you'll have to stay with her, Kit. I've sedated her a bit and I can't do anything more at the moment, but someone ought to sit and watch her, and there's no use depending on the mother.'

Lilli had calmed down, in fact she was finally exhausted and seemed to be sleeping in a hot and fitful way.

'I'll stay,' I said, flattered by Dr Dixon's camaraderie. 'Is it tetanus?' I asked him.

'No. The spasms worried me for a moment. It's a bad case of septicaemia and she may have to lose that leg. It's gangrenous. But she ought to be in hospital, or at least under the kind of constant attention she can't get here. I'll talk to Miss Dalgleish. Do you want me to telephone your mother and tell her you're here, or does she know?'

'No, she doesn't know, but don't telephone before 8.'

'All right. Get a bowl of water and a towel and wash the girl's face. Clean her up a bit. Haven't you got exams — your finals?'

'They start tomorrow,' I said 'I mean the next day.'

'Then see if you can stay here until I can fix something up in the morning. You've been a great help, Kit. Is she your girl?'

I denied it vehemently, and Dr Dixon laughed.

'Honestly,' I insisted. 'It's not me.'

'Is it Devlin, the reporter?'

Everybody knew of Devlin's regular visits to Lilli. It was now a town joke.

'I don't think Lilli's anyone's girl,' I told him.

'Just as well,' the doctor said enigmatically, and he left me watching over Lilli who opened her eyes once, saw me and seemed puzzled, but then closed them again and went back into her hot sleep.

# 18

AT HALF PAST EIGHT IN THE MORNING MISS DALGLEISH ARRIVED with Mr Malone in the Marmon and she called to me before she was in the house, 'Are you in there, Kit?'

'Yes, Miss Dalgleish.'

'Where is she?' Miss Dalgleish demanded as I came out.

'In here,' I told her, pointing to Lilli's room.

'Come along then, Mr Malone,' Miss Dalgleish said and they went into Lilli's room. 'Did she wake up?' she asked me.

'Not really,' I said. 'Just for a moment.'

'Then let's do it quickly,' Miss Dalgleish said. 'Can you lift her, Mr Malone, can you carry her?'

'I think so, Miss Dalgleish, but she looks unconscious.'

'She's asleep,' I told them. Lilli's breathing was deep and exhausted but it was relaxed, and instead of being red and hot her face now looked pale and cold. 'You'll have to keep the blankets on her,' I warned them.

Miss Dalgleish knew why, and as Mr Malone pulled Lilli into a sitting position Miss Dalgleish wrapped the blankets around her and Jackie came in and said: 'Where are you taking her? What are you doing?'

'She has to be looked after,' Miss Dalgleish said. 'She can't stay here.'

I had already warned Jackie, but he didn't like this and he held onto the blankets as Mr Malone began to carry her out. 'You can't take her away,' he said, hanging on.

'Let go,' Miss Dalgleish said. 'Kit, do something.'

'It's all right, Jackie. She has to go.'

'What for?' Jackie said. 'I can look after her.'

'No you can't.'

'You're not taking her to hospital. You're just taking her away.'

Miss Dalgleish ignored him and Mrs Stubeck emerged as Mr Malone was carrying Lilli through the kitchen. Mrs Stubeck knew nothing of what had happened. She had slept through the night, and her first sight of the morning was Lilli in Mr Malone's arms, unconscious, or at least heavily sedated, disappearing into Mr Malone's car.

'That's Lilli,' she said to me.

'Yes, Mrs Stubeck,' I said. 'She's very ill.'

She suddenly got a grip on my arm, a surprisingly strong grip, and I remembered those powerful old punishments the girls, including Lilli, had suffered. 'Why are you taking Lilli away?' she said. 'What's the matter with her?'

'Lilli's very ill,' I said again. 'She's got a poisoned leg and they have to look after her.'

I had not seen Mrs Stubeck for some time, and though I knew she was now permanently in disarray and physically wasted, it shocked me to see her like this. Her eyes were so large and dark-ringed that her sagging face seemed almost black, and though she was wearing a shapeless nightgown I could see that her whole body was bent and emaciated. Her hands were so thin that they looked like Jackie's claws.

'Who's going to make the tea?' she said to me in a complaining voice.

'I don't know, Mrs Stubeck, but Lilli can't.'

'Are they taking her to hospital?'

'I don't know,' I said, and by now Lilli had been put into the back seat of the Marmon. I waited, expecting Miss Dalgleish to come back to talk to us. But she didn't. She got into the back seat and held Lilli up while Jackie made one more desperate attempt to stop them by holding the car door.

'Go away,' Miss Dalgleish said. She closed the door and told Mr Malone to hurry up, and the three of us were left standing at the kitchen door as the Marmon disappeared up the hill.

'Are they going to bring her back tomorrow?' Mrs Stubeck asked me.

'When she's better,' I said.

Mrs Stubeck now began to weep, and for a moment I didn't know what to do. Until now I had been thinking only of Lilli and her rescue, but now that Lilli had been snatched away by Miss Dalgleish my sympathies were suddenly with Mrs Stubeck and Jackie.

Jackie didn't complain or ask what was to become of them. He told me (daring me to challenge him) that he was not going to school that day. 'I'll have to stay and look after her,' he said, nodding in the direction of his mother.

'How?' I asked him. 'What do you think you can do, Jackie?'

'I'll get her a cup of tea ready and some breakfast. I'll cook some lunch. She can't do anything for herself, Kit. She just sits there all day waiting for Lilli.'

'Well Lilli can't help her now,' I told him. 'Lilli needs some real care herself.'

'She'll never come back now, will she?' Jackie said calmly and pushed the last pad of soiled cotton wool into the kitchen stove. 'They're going to cut off her leg, aren't they?'

I denied it, even though I knew what little hope a gangrenous leg had. By now Mrs Stubeck had settled into the kitchen armchair, still wearing her nightgown. She had forgotten me, and with the disgusting smell of burning cotton wool drifting up the hill I went home to explain what had happened, and at the same time persuade my mother that there was nothing she could do for Lilli.

I think I already knew that once those big gates had closed on Lilli Miss Dalgleish would never allow anyone to take her away, so I was not surprised when we heard from Dr Dixon that Miss Dalgleish was nursing Lilli twenty-four hours a day. In fact the treatment itself was very demanding. Lilli's leg had to be drained and kept sterile at all times, which required continuous changing of sterilised cottonwool pads every few hours. And because Miss Dalgleish was devoting herself entirely to Lilli, someone else had to run the house for her, so she sent for Mrs Smythe, the bustler.

It was Miss Dalgleish at her best. The house seemed to

be running smoothly again and Lilli was receiving all the attention she needed. But Miss Dalgleish allowed nobody to see Lilli. 'She has to be kept quiet.' Miss Dalgleish replied to all enquiries. 'She mustn't see anyone.'

'She must be awfully bad,' Dorothy said, 'otherwise I'm sure she would be asking me what has happened to her mother and Jackie.'

In fact my mother had tried to do something about Mrs Stubeck and Jackie, but it was difficult to get around my father.

'Not you,' my father told her. He would defend anyone to the death in a court of law if their rights were threatened, but he was a singular man when it came to his own family. 'You can't take on responsibility for the Stubecks,' he insisted.

Yet it was impossible to leave them alone like that, and though there were quite a few people in town who worried about them the solution for Mrs Stubeck and Jackie was unexpected because it was almost ridiculous. Devlin moved into The Point and took over responsibility for Mrs Stubeck and Jackie. Though the town laughed at the idea, Devlin did it with his usual conviction in conviction itself, so that we soon forgot about Mrs Stubeck and Jackie and waited now to see what would happen to Lilli—locked away behind those high wooden walls.

# 19

DEVLIN HAD BOUGHT HIMSELF A SECOND-HAND MOTORBIKE WITH a sidecar, and the sight of Devlin sitting erect on the old BSA with his arms outstretched and his head in the air and the bike quite beyond him and almost independent of him, was a sight we loved to watch go by. No man had less contact with the machine than Dev, and we always anticipated the bike finally taking him over and doing what it wanted to do. His stare into the distance had no bearing on the road or the corners and the bumps. But Devlin went. And with his conviction in arriving, he arrived.

I haven't mentioned Devlin very much because his visits to The Point had become almost conventional. Until Lilli's illness he had driven down to The Point at least one night a week, and almost every Sunday afternoon. We even got used to seeing Lilli in the sidecar and Jackie on the back of the bike driving out along the Nooah road. The way Lilli rode in that battered sidecar was exactly what we expected of her. She was there without being there, and she was as much out of contact with Devlin on the bike as she was in the house or on the street. Nonetheless she was part of that ensemble, and like Jackie she seemed to enjoy it. Unlike the rest of us Lilli ignored Devlin's hopeless and dangerous incompetence behind the handlebars, and this seemed to me to be something to do with the way they got on with each other.

Devlin had not seen Lilli on the Sunday she became ill because he had been visiting a poultry farmer called Jack Hayes who lived about twenty miles away. Jack was an old rationalist, a follower of Joseph MacCabe and Sir James Fraser, and he and Devlin would quarrel about the pagan societies which Sir James Fraser had analysed in his *Golden Bough*. To Devlin all primitive societies had in them elements of Utopia, and that is what he looked for and found in *The Golden Bough*. Whereas Jack, the rationalist, found proof that all religions and their rituals were based on primitive man's totem system, superstitions and social disciplines. Nonetheless Devlin was in his Uptopian element in that old tin shack which smelled of raw unwashed eggs and chickenfeed, and I still wonder what would have happened to Lilli if Devlin had not been philosophising that day while Lilli was on her bed of pain. How would he have handled it?

In fact it had taken Devlin a week to make up his mind to move in with the Stubecks and during that time other people in town made gestures of help towards Mrs Stubeck and Jackie when they heard about Lilli. She had always had her unknown friends, and what they did for the most part was to take saucepans of food to The Point or old clothes, as if a well-worn jacket or dress would somehow solve the problem. We had two charities in St Helen, both run by different churches, so some of our charitable women organised themselves to visit The Point (my mother told me much later that Miss Dalgleish had alerted them to help Mrs Stubeck).

But there could never be anyone in St Helen who would actually live with Mrs Stubeck and Jackie because The Point was still considered a filthy slum, despite its improvements. And for that matter the Stubecks were still thought of as dirty gypsies. Dorothy Malone would have moved in, but her parents forbade it because she, like me, was sitting for her final exams. Until Devlin moved in Dorothy made almost a daily visit, as I did, and at least we kept the fire going and the dishes washed, and Dorothy did what she could for Mrs Stubeck, even brushing her hair and washing her down.

Devlin's arrival at The Point saved our collective conscience, and after a few days he even had Jackie back at school, the bribe being that Jackie would be taken to school every day on the back of Dev's motorbike. I don't know how he did it but in his gentle way Devlin managed to persuade Mrs Stubeck to dress every morning, and not only did he cook lunch and prepare dinner, he washed clothes and kept the place clean. He was a natural house-wife, despite his personal untidiness, but he got no real help from anyone because the moment he moved into The Point all other charity stopped, as if we had all been relieved of the responsibility. I suppose to that extent the town had complete confidence in Devlin, because we all knew that if Dev had organised himself to do something he would do it.

In fact Dorothy Malone and I also began to ask him about Lilli, because he knew more than we did and we couldn't find out much from Miss Dalgleish. When Dorothy or I telephoned Miss Dalgleish and asked for news we always got the same answer: 'She's very sick and can't talk to you. I'll let you know when she's better. But she is being thoroughly looked after and lacks nothing so you don't have to worry.'

'But what about her leg, Miss Dalgleish?' I would ask.

'It's still draining and it's still very bad. We don't know yet.'

That was all we could get out of her. But Devlin the reporter persisted. He questioned Dr Dixon and Mrs Smythe, the new helper. He asked questions of the chemist who supplied the medicines and the stacks of cottonwool. From Devlin we discovered that Lilli was still rather comatose and flat on her back; that she could only eat light food; that Miss Dalgleish slept in the same room with her; and that Lilli seemed uninterested in anything that was going on around her.

I suppose I worried about Lilli as a friend, but I was now more worried about my exams, and when they were over all I wanted to do was enjoy myself swimming in the river near The Point with not much thought for Lilli except an occasional glance at the house, and a shout or two from Jackie enjoying himself in the shallower water. I knew that my life would go on for ever because our Australian summers were timeless, deathless seasons. I also knew it was my last summer of absolute freedom, and at the time I was in love with a girl named Norma Milton, which was a preoccupation in itself. Nonetheless when Devlin walked over to the swimming hole at The Point and called out to me: 'Kit. Come up when you're through,' I guessed it was something to do with Lilli, so I left Norma and the river and walked up to the house.

'You can see Lilli on Sunday,' he told me. 'Miss Dalgleish told me to tell you, and your friend Dorothy. You'll have to go together if you want to see her.'

Had Devlin seen Lilli?

'No. Miss Dalgleish won't let me in. She's very stubborn.' Which was as near as Devlin could come to a criticism because he never criticised anyone.

'I suppose that means Lilli's getting better,' I said.

'She can't sit up yet,' Devlin said, 'but she's out of danger.'

'Does that mean she won't lose her leg?'

'It's still not better, Kit. That's all I know.'

I telephoned Dorothy that night and Dorothy told me she had already made arrangements for us to visit Lilli at 3 o'clock that Sunday.

'We can only stay half an hour, Kit. And Miss Dalgleish wouldn't let me talk to her on the phone.'

On Sunday we rang the outside bell but the big gate was not locked and, when we walked inside, Miss Dalgleish was waiting for us leaning on her stick at the front door, with a clean and sparkling Tilley barking at our feet.

'Good afternoon, Dorothy. Good afternoon, Kit,' she said. 'If you give me those I'll put them in water.'

Dorothy was holding a bunch of flowers. I had nothing because I had resisted my mother's suggestions to take Lilli a bag of peaches. 'Miss Dalgleish has everything Lilli needs,' I said, 'and I doubt if Lilli can eat peaches anyway.'

Dorothy reluctantly handed over the flowers and Miss Dalgleish took us into the salon and told us to sit down for a moment.

'I must ask you to be careful what you say to Lilli,' she said. 'She will ask about her mother and her brother. I have told her that they are being well looked after. I have spoken to Mister Devlin on the phone and he says they are all right, which is all she needs to know.'

'How is her leg?' Dorothy asked.

'It will be a long time healing, but she won't lose it.'

'Thank heaven for that,' Dorothy said.

I had been standing to one side listening and at the same time surreptitiously watching Miss Dalgleish. She looked erect and alert, as if the effort of looking after Lilli had restored some hidden healthy reserves she seemed for a while to have lost. She was still in complete control, in fact she seemed to have gone back a few years to the Miss Dalgleish who had run this house and supervised Lilli's schoolgirl life as if destiny itself was on her side. I suppose if I had known about Miss Dalgleish's real condition I would probably have recognised it as a sad little Indian summer that was certain to be short-lived.

'Did you do well in your exams, Kit?' she asked me.

'I don't think so,' I said because I didn't want to talk about it.

When she asked Dorothy the same question as we walked slowly up the stairs behind her Dorothy smiled at me and said, 'I'm like Kit, Miss Dalgleish. I'm superstitious, so I don't want to even answer that question.'

'You are both very intelligent,' Miss Dalgleish said impatiently, 'so you'll both do well.'

I think if I had stepped straight from The Point into Lilli's room the effect on me wouldn't have been so bad. But these little preliminaries with Miss Dalgleish had already put Lilli into some sort of helpless condition, and what followed was a confirmation of the way I felt as I walked into the little bedroom.

Lilli was lying flat on her back. Though I had last seen her in a coma she had still been, even in her fever, the inexhaustible girl I had always known. But Lilli like this looked beaten. She was pale and very still, and even in the way she was lying she seemed to be concentrating on something else. In difficulty, Lilli had always closed herself off from everything, as if whatever was happening to her was nothing to do with anyone but herself, and that was what Lilli was doing now. She wore a white lawn nightgown and a short lace jacket, which was so unlike Lilli that I noticed the clothes almost before I noticed

Lilli. The room, which smelled heavily of disinfectant and iodine, was rather cool and dark because recuperation in those days suggested drawn curtains. They were not drawn, but that subdued, summery light concentrated the stifling air of invalid sickness in the room, and hovering over it was that powerful angel Miss Dalgleish.

'Hello, Lill,' Dorothy said, and I mumbled something myself.

Lilli glanced at Miss Dalgleish before she said 'Hello' to us, and it was obvious that she was aware of being watched and listened-to by Miss Dalgleish.

'You can talk about exams,' Miss Dalgleish said.

Was she telling us what to talk about, or telling Lilli? Obviously she was telling Dorothy and me, and I knew then that our visit was Miss Dalgleish's idea, not Lilli's. Lilli, lying stiff and white and withdrawn didn't want to see anyone, I knew it at a glance.

Dorothy felt the same way, and for a moment she didn't know what to say. Then she said rather hurriedly, as if she had to fill the empty space between us: 'The exams were awful, Lill. I could only answer five of the maths' questions, and I hadn't read a word about Pitt's plan for a Federated Europe after the war of the Third Coalition.'

Lilli didn't answer but she looked quickly from Dorothy to me, and those quick sharp glances were the only real response that she seemed willing to share with us.

Dorothy touched my arm lightly as if to warn me that we must be careful, and that somehow we ought to relax. 'How are you anyway, Lilli?' she said now, and she sat on the edge of the bed.

'Don't sit on the bed, Dorothy,' Miss Dalgleish said. 'You might touch her leg.'

'Oh, I'm sorry,' Dorothy said. 'I forgot.'

'Sit in the chairs,' Miss Dalgleish told us, and she pointed to two chairs, one each side of the bed.

Dorothy and I sat down; by now I felt very subdued by Miss Dalgleish whereas Dorothy the nun had become her usual, smiling self, and she asked Lilli again how she was.

'I'm all right,' Lilli said with another sharp glance at Dorothy. 'Just flat on my back.'

'We kept hearing awful things,' Dorothy told her.

'I suppose you did,' Lilli said. 'But I didn't know much about it.'

'What does the doctor say?' Dorothy asked her.

This time Lilli looked at Miss Dalgleish before replying and she said, 'I have to stay here until my leg gets better.'

'How long will that be?'

'I'm not sure . . .' Lilli was frowning, and she was so reluctant to talk about it that we knew the whole conversation was distasteful to her. 'He doesn't know how long.'

'Is it painful?'

'No.'

'You were lucky Kit was there,' Dorothy said.

'Dr Dixon told me,' Lilli said and glanced quickly at me as if that one glance would say all that she would never say.

I knew now that she wouldn't ask me about her mother and Jackie so I told her that they were all right, and that Devlin was doing a marvellous job looking after them.

'Yes, I know that,' she said.

'Do you want Kit or me to do anything for them, Lilli?' Dorothy asked her.

'No,' Lilli said. 'They're all right.'

It was too much for Dorothy who was more affected than I was by Lilli's reserve. Dorothy was a polite girl, but her cheerful, gentle, all-embracing affection gave her more courage than I had, and she said to Miss Dalgleish: 'Couldn't we see Lilli alone for a little while, Miss Dalgleish. We're much better when it's just the three of us together.'

Miss Dalgleish stiffened for a moment as if she was suddenly aware of our brutal little compact—our ruthlessly young faces and childish secrets. Dorothy didn't mean it that way but that was how it affected Miss Dalgleish.

'All right, Dorothy,' she said. 'I think I can trust you both not to tire Lilli, so I'll leave you. But only for ten minutes.'

Lilli watched her go and, now that we were free of that persistent shadow, Dorothy said softly, 'Surely there's something we can do, Lilli.'

Lilli shook her head just a little. 'No,' she said. 'There's nothing you can do. I don't need anything.'

But Dorothy persisted. She said she would come and read to Lilli, and though Lilli didn't resist the idea she didn't really respond to it. Dorothy went on talking about school, the teachers, the other girls, her mother, and finally, hesitantly, she told Lilli that she would be leaving St Helen at the end of the summer.

'I'll be going to the Sisters of Mercy at Castlemaine,' Dorothy said.

Lilli's cat's eyes suddenly looked accusingly at Dorothy, but she didn't say anything.

'I'm sorry, Lilli. I shouldn't have told you,' Dorothy said.

I knew that Lilli didn't want to talk at all, but with Dorothy she had to talk. 'I thought you were going to wait for a year,' she said to Dorothy.

'I know. But they want to make me a teacher, so they say I shouldn't interrupt my studies.'

Lilli tried to raise herself a little. 'So you won't be a nun,' she said.

'I'll still be a nun. But I was given the choice of studying for mission work or teaching, and I prefer teaching. So I'll be a student novice at first, and after that . . .'

Lilli fell back again and Dorothy's cheerful face was so unhappy now that it was obviously time for me to leave them alone because I knew that these two had their own language, their own loyalties, and always that marvellous faith they had somehow sustained in each other from the first day of their commitment in 'Boom' MacGill's class.

'I'll leave you to your joy and your misery,' I said, getting up. It was a poor attempt to be light-hearted, but it was the best I could do and they didn't suggest that I stay.

'You're not leaving St Helen, too, are you Kit?' Lilli said.

'I don't think so,' I said. 'There's nothing for me to leave for.'

'Yes . . .' Lilli said, and added almost dreamily and quite enigmatically: 'It's summer.'

I waited, but there was nothing more I could say now except 'Goodbye, Lilli.'

She watched me go without a word and only said 'Goodbye, Kit,' as I closed the door.

Once outside I had to recover from the curious atmosphere of that room. It had been so stringent and confined that I was glad to leave it. In fact I was relieved to find Tilley when I went downstairs. He tried to reach my hand for affection as I called out to Miss Dalgleish that I was going.

'Just a moment, Kit,' she said, coming out of the library with her spectacles on. 'Come in here, please. I want to talk to you.'

I followed her into the library and I noticed that Lilli's desk still had her schoolbooks on it, not only her textbooks but her half-filled exercise books.

After Lilli's room I was glad to be facing Miss Dalgleish, although her first question surprised me. 'Tell me, Kit. Is Mr Devlin a clean person?' she asked me as she pointed to the big leather couch and then told me to sit down.

The last time I had seen Devlin at The Point he had been standing outside the kitchen door stripped to the waist. He was scrubbing himself with soap and water and dousing his arms and washing his face and hair with the sort of conviction that Devlin's perfectly clean world was made of.

'He's a fanatic,' I told Miss Dalgleish. 'Probably the cleanest person in town.'

'He wants to come and see Lilli, but I don't want him bringing any germs with him from that terrible house. He's so untidy,' she said.

'That doesn't mean he isn't clean, Miss Dalgleish,' I said.

'Dr Dixon said they were handling horse manure.'

'That's Jackie,' I told her.

'That boy . . .' She took off her spectacles. 'Last week that little boy got over the fence and tried to steal Tilley. Go outside,' Miss Dalgleish told the dog sharply.

Tilley stayed stubbornly at my feet.

Miss Dalgleish sighed and ignored him and then told me that she wanted me to do something for her. 'Will you bring me Lilli's clothes,' she said.

'You mean from The Point?' I asked.

'Of course,' she said. 'I could have asked Dorothy to do

it but I don't like to ask her to go into that house, and in any case she couldn't carry them.'

'What clothes do you want?' I asked her.

'All of them,' Miss Dalgleish said. 'Will you get them for me?'

'Does Lilli want them?' I asked.

'What do you mean, Kit?'

'She didn't mention it.'

'She doesn't have to mention it. She's going to need them eventually. I would sooner ask you to bring them than someone else.'

'Devlin could bring them,' I said. 'He's got a motorbike.'

'I don't want to ask him. I am asking you.'

I knew that Miss Dalgleish was really asking me to take sides. Lilli was not going back to The Point, that was obvious. Miss Dalgleish now had all the advantages, and she was not going to give them up. But face to face with her I was something of a coward and I knew that I couldn't say no to her. In fact I didn't want to say no. If I had to make a choice for Lilli I knew I would leave her there. She was not only better off, but The Point had always been an aberration which gave Lilli nothing and took away everything. Sitting here in this rich little library, I could even forget about Jackie and Mrs Stubeck and Devlin.

'All right,' I said. 'I'll bring them tomorrow night.'

'Lilli will be grateful,' Miss Dalgleish told me.

But as I left I felt very depressed. That room had told me all that I needed to know about Lilli lying in bed for weeks, half conscious and helpless, while Miss Dalgleish not only acted as nurse and changed soiled bandages but also washed her and gave her bedpans (I had seen one under the bed) and changed her nightgown and brushed her hair, fed her, read to her, and barely left her side day and night. And it seemed to me that Lilli, lying there like that, had lost almost every one of the disciplines she had lived by. Her self-sufficiency had been taken away from her for the first time in her life, and so far she didn't seem to know how to get it back.

# 20

I THOUGHT OF IT AS SOMETHING MISS DALGLEISH HAD FINALLY won and as some sort of life force that Lilli had lost, and as they locked themselves up once more with their silent tensions and unspoken differences Lilli simply did as she was told. She was not resentful, she didn't object, and above all she didn't contribute. But even Dorothy Malone recognised the result. Unlike me, Dorothy didn't look for Greek drama in what was happening in that household, but she said to me after her second visit to Lilli: 'She'll never go back to The Point, Kit.'

'How do you know?' I asked her. 'Did she tell you?'

'No, of course not. But I know . . .'

'She can't leave Devlin down there for ever,' I said.

'I don't think she even cares, which is not like her.'

'She'll get over it,' I said.

'I don't think so,' Dorothy told me.

I didn't think so either, and now my fickle sympathies were with Devlin and Jackie and Mrs Stubeck, and it was Devlin who had my admiration. He had helped me collect Lilli's clothes (neatly stacked in her new chest of drawers) and even when he realised I was taking all of them he didn't question me or try to stop me. I felt guilty about it and I was glad when Miss Dalgleish simply took the old leather suitcase (covered with labels from Carlsbad, Vienna, Paris, Salzburg, Innsbruck and Garmisch-Partenkirchen) and didn't ask me to go up to see Lilli. I no longer wanted to see her in her present condition.

I did wonder what on earth Devlin and Lilli said to each other when Miss Dalgleish finally let him in. Lilli doesn't mention it in her black book, and when I went down to The Point and sat in the kitchen and asked

Devlin how she was he said: 'She told me to take Tilley back with me.'

'The dog?'

'Yes.'

'Did you?'

'Yes, of course I did.'

'I'm surprised that Miss Dalgleish didn't object,' I told him.

'Maybe she did. I don't know what she and Lilli said to each other, Kit, but when I told her what Lilli wanted she went upstairs and came down after a few minutes and said, "Take him" so I did.'

'But how was Lilli?'

Devlin was like Lilli—you could never tell what he was thinking or feeling, and above all he never exposed himself. But whereas Lilli defended herself by force of arms, Devlin was hard to find behind his innocence. He gazed at me with his pale blue eyes and I knew he couldn't tell me what I wanted to know about Lilli because he didn't know himself. All that Devlin would allow to penetrate his innocent armour was the simple fact that Lilli was lying in bed when she shouldn't be.

'Do you know anything about Joseph Priestley, Kit?' he asked me.

'Only that he discovered oxygen, if that's the one you mean.'

'That's the one. But Priestley was also a natural philosopher and he said that the body is constructed as a perfect state but only if you force it to function. Lilli shouldn't be lying down. She should be trying to get up.'

'Maybe Dr Dixon told her to stay down.'

'I told Dr Dixon he was wrong.'

I laughed. 'What did he say?'

Devlin was very serious. 'I wouldn't repeat it,' he said.

'Did you tell Lilli that she ought to get up?' I asked him.

'Of course I did.'

'Well did she?'

Devlin shook his head. 'Lilli will get up when she wants to,' he said, and he asked me if I had ever heard of Priestley's eudemonism.

'No,' I said. 'What is it?'

'It's a theory that the greatest individual happiness is only compatible with the happiness of other men. It was the Greeks who thought it up,' he said.

'What's that got to do with Lilli?'

Devlin looked surprised. 'Nothing,' he said.

'I thought you were making a point about Lilli lying down.'

'I had finished with that,' Devlin said, which was typical of Devlin's kind of conversation. He was sometimes so oblique and tangential that you didn't know whether he was continuing a subject or starting something new.

By now I had become almost as interested in Devlin as I was in Lilli, because he had made such a routine of his responsibility for Jackie and Mrs Stubeck that I could easily imagine him living at The Point and looking after them long after Lilli had recovered and forgotten them — if that was the way it was going to happen. But it was not quite like that.

Knowing that Lilli didn't really want to see me I didn't go back to Miss Dalgleish's. But Dorothy did and Devlin did, and I followed Lilli's recovery through them, though only in the thin space between my own problems. I was now finished with school. I had passed reasonably well, and it only remained for me to live out the long hot summer before I did something with myself — if there was anything to do. Most of the youth in our town were unemployed and so far I was no exception. We were a depressed town in the middle of a depression, so Lilli didn't figure too largely in my interest, except that my curiosity about what was happening to her was too strong to ignore because I knew that the Greek drama going on in that house was by no means over.

But whereas I was full of admiration for Devlin's behaviour, most of the town was full of admiration for Miss Dalgleish's selfless devotion, and the old mystery of what went on behind those wooden walls was still as fascinating as ever, because there were still so many questions unanswered about Lilli. In fact they remained unanswerable as long as Lilli was unseen and unseeable. What bothered me (and Dorothy) was how little sympathy there was for Lilli, which was probably Lilli's own fault because she had always resisted sympathy in the past. Why should she get it now? So there was a curious sort of resentment among some of the town gossips that Lilli should by lying in that bed at all. She ought to be back at The Point with her mother and her brother. That was where she belonged. After all she was still a Stubeck and a gypsy.

Then one day I met Dorothy on the dirt road that led to The Point and she told me that Lilli could now hobble around on crutches, a few steps anyway, and that she was finally on the way to real recovery.

'So maybe she'll think about going back to The Point,' I said. Dorothy shook her head. 'It's very unlikely, Kit,' she told me rather sadly. 'Lilli's simply locked herself up in that house.' It was the same phrase I had thought of myself, so I knew what she meant.

I was on my way to swim near The Point because it was over a hundred degrees in the shade, but Dorothy had never been seen swimming. She was for ever in preparation for her one and only vocation and was always fully dressed. Dorothy was on her way to The Point to see Mrs Stubeck.

'Devlin says she's not very well,' she told me.

'Does Lilli ask about her?'

'She doesn't ask me, but I know Devlin tells her what is happening.'

'Well, at least Jackie is all right,' I said. I knew that Jackie was scavenging the town as usual, and that Devlin didn't interfere.

'Jackie is just like Lilli in a way,' Dorothy said. 'He can always look after himself. It's Mrs Stubeck I'm worried about.'

I went on down to the river and stripped to my bathing suit and was deep in a hole among the fifty people crowded into our river when I saw Dorothy running around the barbed wire fence to the bank waving to me.

'Come quick, Kit,' she was shouting. 'Something's happened.'

I swam ashore and began to dry myself so that I could

put my trousers on, but she waved her arms and said. 'Never mind that,' so I followed her back to The Point as I was. As I caught up with her she stopped, breathless, and held my arm.

'I think Mrs Stubeck is dead,' she said.

I don't know why, but the first thing I said was: 'Where's Jackie?'

'Isn't he swimming?' Dorothy said.

The swimming hole was packed with boys, girls, youths and adults, and I hadn't looked for him.

'I suppose he is,' I said. 'Are you sure about Mrs Stubeck?'

'I don't know. That's why I called you.'

I had no desire to stare death in its yellow, ugly face, but Dorothy shamed me and I went with her into the barren little room. As soon as I was adjusted to the dim light inside after the hot glare outside I could see Mrs Stubeck lying outstretched on her bed with her flaccid arms out of the covers and a smooth and relaxed and utterly empty expression on her dark, waxlike face.

'She's so cold,' Dorothy said.

I had never seen death before but I knew it, and I turned away and got out of that room as quickly as I could.

'She's dead,' I said to Dorothy and she followed me.

'What are we going to do?' Dorothy asked me.

'Dev should be home any minute now,' I said.

'You mean we should just wait for him?'

'No. I'll go and get Dr Dixon,' I said. 'You wait here for Dev.'

'What about Jackie?'

'He can't do anything,' I said. 'Leave him.'

'But he's playing.'

'What difference does it make?' I said angrily, because anger seemed to be the only way I had of coping with death. 'He'll find out soon enough.'

'All right,' she said. 'But hurry.'

I dressed now and ran up the hill and along the main street to Dr Dixon's house, and just before I got there I saw Devlin on his motorbike on the way to The Point. I shouted to him and waved. Head in the air, eyes on some eventual point of arrival, Devlin didn't see me and rode on.

Mrs Dixon answered the doorbell, and when I told her in something of a hot and breathless panic (I had been running) that Mrs Stubeck was dead and 'Where is Dr Dixon?', she asked me if I was sure.

'Yes, I've seen her,' I said.

'Is there anybody with her?' she asked.

'Dorothy Malone,' I said. 'And I think Devlin is there by now.'

When Dr Dixon came out and said roughly, 'Well, Kit, you're at it again,' I felt somewhat better. He told me to go back and tell Devlin and Dorothy that he would be there in an hour. 'Tell them to pull the blinds down and shut the door to keep the room cool,' he said. 'And if they don't need you, Kit, go home. Don't hang around the place.'

I hardly needed that advice. I ran back to The Point and when I arrived, red and sweating, Devlin was walking back from the river with Jackie.

'He said that Jackie ought to know,' Dorothy said to me. 'There's no use hiding it.'

'Maybe he's right,' I said, and I told Dorothy what to do about the room and waited for her to do it because I was not going in there again. Jackie, dressed in clinging black drawers and with Tilley behind him, was still wet when he arrived with Devlin, and he asked Dorothy where Lilli was.

'She still can't walk, Jackie.'

'Isn't she coming back?'

'She can't come back. Not at the moment anyway.'

Though Devlin had told him he didn't ask about his mother. He wasn't crying, and he didn't look as if he expected any pity. But he wouldn't go near the house.

'I'm not going in there any more,' he said, and he turned around and ran back to the river with Tilley at his heels.

We watched him go as if he had left us there with something that didn't belong to any of us.

'Poor Jackie,' Dorothy said. 'He doesn't understand.'

But I knew that he understood. Jackie had decided it was no use bothering about death without Lilli.

'What about Lilli?' I said to Devlin.

'I'll tell her what's happened,' Devlin said. 'There's nothing you can do about it, Kit, so why don't you go home.'

I couldn't go back to the swimming hole so I went home, leaving Devlin and Dorothy standing in the faint summer dusk outside the kitchen door waiting for Dr Dixon. Like Jackie they didn't want to go into the house, and I doubted if I should ever want to go in there again myself.

# 21

I SUPPOSE THE TOWN'S MAIN INTEREST IN MRS STUBECK'S DEATH was what Lilli would do about it. Dorothy had taken Jackie home with her because he refused to sleep in the house without Lilli and said he would spend the night on the river bank. But it was Devlin who made all the arrangements for the funeral, and it was soon clear that Miss Dalgleish was paying for it. The real problem was religion. Who would conduct the service? Mrs Stubeck had never been seen inside a church, although in the early days of their arrival in town she was once seen with Lilli and baby Jackie outside the Methodist Church on a Sunday, more or less begging.

We still knew nothing about Lilli except that Devlin had obviously spoken to her, and it was decided that the ceremony would be conducted by the Presbyterian Minister, the Reverend Armitage. This suggested Miss Dalgleish's influence.

The funeral was the best that could be expected of a Stubeck occasion in our town. The only people who followed the hearse on that hot summer's day were myself on a bicycle, Devlin and barefooted Jackie and Tilley on the motorbike, and Dorothy, Miss Dalgleish and Lilli in Mr Malone's Marmon. At The Point Lilli did not get out of the car. She had not looked at her mother's body, nor had Jackie. When the procession set off I was at the tail end of it as it went up the hill and skirted the edges of the town to follow the sandy perimeter of the racecourse which also contained the golf-links and beyond it the cemetery. We said in our town that the three deadly sins of St Helen could all be buried in the same place.

When we arrived at the cemetery, and the coffin was unloaded by the four volunteers from Mr Ransom's undertaking business, we had to walk a long way to the grave. I don't know what we expected of Lilli, but we were more interested in watching her emerge from the Marmon. She refused all help and, with a pair of heavy wooden crutches, she followed the coffin in and out of the gravestones and the spiky clumps of Phoenix grass that always thrived in the cemetery, summer or winter. Lilli was dressed in black (how had Miss Dalgleish managed that in a day?) and she was an extraordinary figure because she was so pale that inside a soft black dress she looked more like a gypsy than she had when she was brown and healthy. I think it was her black cat's eyes and black hair that were given sudden emphasis, but there was also something rather wild in Lilli as if (like me) she was angry with death or with herself or with nature or with the grass or with everybody around her.

We stood around the empty grave while the coffin (painted black) was lowered on its straps. Lilli leaned on her crutches and said something briefly to Jackie who was standing beside her, one bare foot on the other. Everything was awkward, we were such a mismatched lot. The Reverend Armitage, who was usually a ferocious evangelist for death as for life, almost mumbled the ceremony as if he wasn't interested in it. Miss Dalgleish leaned on her stick with Mr Malone behind her, apparently ready to hold her if she needed holding. Dorothy and I were standing together. We both watched Lilli who did not weep or show any sign of emotion and seemed only to be waiting, as if all this was nothing to do with any of us. She ignored us. After the ceremony she didn't wait but turned around and hobbled back to the car. When Tilley tried to get in with her she threw him out and sat stiff and erect in the back seat with Miss Dalgleish as Mr Malone drove them away.

# 22

TWO DAYS AFTER THE FUNERAL, AT 5 O'CLOCK IN THE EVENING, Lilli arrived back at The Point on Devlin's motorbike. She was sitting in the sidecar nursing her crutches, and on the back of the bike behind Devlin was the old, leather suitcase belonging to Miss Dalgleish that I had packed Lilli's clothes in when I delivered them to the old lady.

I was fishing a little further up the river with Jackie. Or rather Jackie and Tilley had joined me, and we both stood up to watch when we saw the motorbike arriving and recognised the passenger.

'It's Lilli and her crutches,' Jackie said.

We watched her struggling to get out of the sidecar which had no door, and because she couldn't do it without Devlin's help and because he was so awkward she simply fell out of the sidecar and landed on her back. I winced, but Jackie laughed.

'It looks like she's moved back,' I said to him.

'She must have got out when the old lady wasn't looking,' Jackie said.

'Why do you say that?' I asked him.

'The old lady had her locked up, Kit,' he said. 'She wouldn't let Lilli go.'

Miss Dalgleish's hold on Lilli had always been physical as far as Jackie was concerned. I suppose that was the only way he could understand it. But I wondered how Lilli had escaped the real hold that Miss Dalgleish had on her.

'Did you know she was coming back?' I asked Jackie because he now settled down to his fishing as if he had expected Lilli.

'Not me,' Jackie said.

I didn't believe him. I was fairly sure that Lilli had told him she was coming back when she spoke to him at the funeral. She had probably made up her mind even then, and though I didn't know what had changed Lilli's attitude, it was obvious that her mother's death had somehow cut her loose again from Miss Dalgleish.

I didn't go into the house when we returned to The Point, but Devlin was outside stoking a fire in the old oil drum they used as an incinerator. Lilli was in her mother's room; the window was open and I could see her sitting on the bed. When she heard Jackie talking to Devlin she called out: 'Come in here, Jackie. I want you.'

'What for?' Jackie said suspiciously.

'Never mind. Come in here.'

'What for?' Jackie said again.

'Jackie. Come in here,' Lilli said, and Jackie obeyed.

I wanted to ask Devlin quietly what had happened between Lilli and Miss Dalgleish, but all I managed to ask was 'What's she doing?'

'She wants to burn everything,' Devlin said.

Almost immediately Jackie came to the window and pushed out a bundle of clothes. I recognised Mrs Stubeck's new dress and shoes and filthy slippers, and some of the old clothes our charitable women had given her. There were also a few old rags of cotton shifts and stockings and black dresses, and a shiny black straw hat with a chewed brim. They were all soiled, and so were the two sheets which were so filthy and stained that even Devlin's house-wifery must have been beaten by them.

I didn't offer to help and Devlin lifted them all up with a stick to feed them to the flames. Then Lilli appeared at the kitchen door without her crutches, hopping on one leg and leaning against the doorjamb. She held a small wooden box in her hand.

'Put that on the fire will you, Kit,' she said to me, since I was nearest to her, and even in that casual instruction I recognised the resurrection of the old Lilli.

The box looked like the sort our schools kept chalk in. It had a sliding lid. It too was stained and dirty and I guessed that it held whatever valuables Mrs Stubeck had accumulated in her lifetime as a gypsy. It was too tempting to resist the information, and instead of putting it on the fire unopened I slid open the lid and took out the items one by one to feed to the flames.

I didn't learn much, but I learned something. The first thing I took out was some sort of magistrate's summons. I couldn't inspect it properly, but I guessed it was the one that had finally put Matty in jail. There were folded letters which I opened as I tossed them in. They were written in a childish hand on yellowing, broken paper, almost illegible now. And there were half a dozen photographs. The top one was obviously of Grace or Pansy or Alice, playing the fool on a beach with a man. There was a photograph of a grave, and one of a very young Matty dressed as a jockey mounted on a spindly-looking horse. There was also a dog-eared photograph of Mrs Stubeck in a big floppy hat looking young, plump, and very gypsy-like. And finally an old photograph, almost a daguerreotype, of a stone house that was obviously in some village in Wales or Ireland or Scotland. I couldn't read the name but I threw it in. The last item in the box was a bundle of papers tied with string and for a moment I thought of telling Lilli it might be birth certificates, but I knew Lilli didn't want to know what was in the box so I threw it in and the box after it.

'Is that all?' Devlin said to Lilli.

'Yes,' Lilli said, and by now there was more foul-smelling smoke than flame, although Devlin kept stirring the fire and he had not yet put in the sheets.

'Did you get any fish?' Lilli asked me as I tried to avoid the smoke.

'Five or six,' I said. 'Do you want them?'

She shook her head and turned around to hop inside again. 'Goodbye, Kit,' she said in her usual dismissal when she did not want to talk or answer questions.

'S'long Lilli,' I said, and as I walked home up the hill, thinking that everything suddenly looked as if it were back to normal for Lilli, I knew it was by no means so because there was still the problem of Miss Dalgleish.

The next day, Lilli simply returned to her routine of

housekeeping for Miss Dalgleish. Devlin, who had gone back to his boarding house, picked her up in the morning on his motorbike and delivered her on her crutches to the big wooden gate. He collected her again at 5 o'clock and took her back to The Point; once again this became the routine, as if nothing had interrupted it.

But if this was Lilli's way of rescuing herself it must have meant something else to Miss Dalgleish, because her final dissolution began when Lilli returned to The Point. I don't suppose we noticed it at first because we didn't see much of Miss Dalgleish. What we noticed was their behaviour as they walked down the street on Saturday mornings. Lilli was soon off her crutches and walking with a stick, and it seemed at first as if Miss Dalgleish had re-emerged for Lilli's sake.

They were an extraordinary sight as they closed the big gates behind them and began their slow walk (both with sticks) to the shops and Post Office. They seemed utterly unaware of anyone else but themselves, as if they were so trapped in each other's company that even a walk down the street was something to do with the curious grip they had on each other. They rarely spoke, that was normal, and if they did it was almost with the same kind of voice, because Lilli was behaving more and more like Miss Dalgleish. But it was difficult to know who was leading whom. Like two people dancing a foxtrot one had to lead and the other had to follow, and as Lilli was limping badly it was Miss Dalgleish who made the pace for her. But as Lilli became more robust we began to notice that Miss Dalgleish had to be waited for. It was Lilli who then adjusted her pace to the old lady. It was Lilli who did the shopping and made the decisions, and when there was no other interpretation to put on it Miss Dalgleish gave up her Saturday excursions and disappeared once more behind her high wooden walls.

If we had known that Miss Dalgleish was dying we might have been more curious about her condition. But we still thought her indestructible, and we were so used to her secretive life that we didn't know that she was deteriorating a little every day, so that Lilli's role as housekeeper and nurse and authority developed almost imperceptibly as the weeks passed. When Lilli was able to walk or limp without her stick, Mrs Smythe found herself out of a job. Lilli didn't need her. After that, the only outsiders who knew first-hand what went on in that house were old Dr Wallace and Dorothy Malone. Nobody else was allowed in and anything I knew came from Dorothy who warned me not to tell anyone.

'I can tell it to you, Kit, but Lilli would never forgive me if it got around.'

'If what gets around?' I said.

'I don't know. The way they live in there.'

'How do they live? Is it any different?'

'Well, Miss Dalgleish is now more or less confined to her chair. She can get up and downstairs once a day, but that's about all. The rest of the time she spends sitting in the library.'

'What does Lilli do?'

'Everything. She arrives every morning at 8 o'clock, she helps Miss Dalgleish to dress, she gets the breakfast, cleans the house, cooks the meals and runs the place. And once you're in there, Kit, the outside world simply doesn't exist.'

'It was always like that,' I pointed out.

'I know. But even more so now, because Miss Dalgleish is entirely dependent on Lilli.'

At this stage Lilli still didn't know that Miss Dalgleish's situation was hopeless (Dorothy told me this later), and even when Miss Dalgleish became worse Lilli simply thought of it as the symptom of a long and heavy illness, rather than a quick and fatal one. But it is hard to say what Lilli thought or understood, because she doesn't mention it in her black book. Her information about Miss Dalgleish and herself becomes rather sparse at the end of her notes.

From outside we knew that Miss Dalgleish was in serious trouble when Lilli finally abandoned The Point and moved herself back to the old house. That sort of transformation always meant a big decision for Lilli, but it was Dorothy who told me the reason for it. Miss Dalgleish could no longer be left at night. She could no longer get down the stairs, and Lilli had called in Devlin to help her shift the spare bed from her own bedroom (where Miss Dalgleish had set it up with the help of Dr Dixon and the gardener) to Miss Dalgleish's room.

Lilli's authority now became absolute. Miss Dalgleish had no relatives at hand to play any part in her care. I remembered an old and very bald cousin from Melbourne visiting her once in a blue Rolls Royce, and there was always talk of Dalgleish nephews who were well-known in Sydney and Adelaide and Melbourne because they were on the other side of the family, the more powerful and more fashionable side. But they had never visited Miss Dalgleish. Her way of life was now ordered by Lilli and old Dr Wallace and J. C. Strapp, her solicitor who looked after her affairs and was now seen coming and going through the big gates. I suppose Dr Wallace and Strapp could have called in a nurse and another housekeeper, but Miss Dalgleish must have given them strict instructions no to do so: to leave it to Lilli. Lilli was now fulfilling her true destiny, or rather the destiny that Miss Dalgleish had arranged for her from the outset. She would be there at the end when Miss Dalgleish needed her.

But once again Lilli showed us it was not servitude. A few days after she had moved back to the old house we realised that Jackie was there too. He had finally joined that little community behind those high wooden walls, and Dorothy told us that he was actually sleeping in Lilli's bedroom now that Lilli had moved in with Miss Dalgleish. There was a certain irony in the situation because the curious and the gossips who wanted to know about Miss Dalgleish would stop Jackie to ask about her. But Jackie's only answer was 'I don't know. I don't see the old lady.' Jackie became the messenger: to the shops, the chemist, the Post Office, and even to the bank for money. We never saw Lilli, not even on Saturday mornings. She was locked up again, but this time with a predestination that had long ago been waiting for her.

'It's terribly sad,' Dorothy told me. 'Miss Dalgleish clings to her. I mean with her eyes. She can't move much, but Lilli reads to her for hours, and they've moved the gramophone upstairs, so its a sort of endless attachment between them. They hardly talk to each other, they're still extraordinarily stiff and cold, but they always seem to know what to expect of each other, the way they always did. Only now Miss Dalgleish is dying, Kit, and Lilli knows it.'

I remember that last week very well because it started for me with Devlin (as usual) on the street corner now reaching the end of his interminable lecture on Utopia. He had finally come to the Sermon on the Mount, and though I had been given a fairly sound education in the New Testament, I had never heard Matthew, Chapter V, recited the way Devlin did it that day, as if it was no more than another model for a Utopian future that might easily work if it was ever given a chance. To Devlin, Christ's words were not an outline of the Christian faith; they were rather a declaration of a possible system, and he made each point as if it ought to be tried out somewhere. After all—blessed were the poor, for their's shall be the kingdom of heaven. Wasn't that the foundation of the Utopian idea? He went on with Christ's blessings for the meek, the righteous, the merciful and the pure in heart. Weren't these the virtues of those men who were the very salt of the earth? And wasn't the perfect moral advice for an ideal society that remarkable instruction of Christ's—to turn the other cheek?

They were the last words we would hear from Devlin on that corner because Jackie arrived to tell him that Lilli wanted him, 'Quick!' Jackie nudged me with his doubled-up fingers and said, 'Lilli told me if I saw you, Kit, to bring you as well.'

'What for?'

'How do I know? But she said to hurry.'

With Jackie behind him on the motorbike and myself in the sidecar Devlin roared down the main street to the old house. Jackie had the key to the big gate, and when we went inside the house I could see that all the lights were on from top to bottom.

'They're here,' Jackie shouted from the foot of the stairs.

Lilli came down the stairs and stared at us for a moment as if we were out of place there. She looked almost perfect in the neatness and care of her hair and her dress and her shoes, and it seemed to me to be deliberate.

'I want you to carry Miss Dalgleish down to the library,' she said. 'So come upstairs.' And as we followed her up the stairs she said to Jackie: 'You come and carry the pillow.'

We didn't ask questions, we obeyed, and when I walked behind her into Miss Dalgleish's bedroom I had the peculiar feeling that this had somehow become Lilli's house, even when I saw Miss Dalgleish lying in her brass bed and saw around her the accumulation of a rich spinster's life which had been lived in another world rather than the one outside on our street. There were more modern French paintings on the walls, lovely silk Japanese prints, expensive bibelots, small sculptures on the mantlepiece and dozens of framed photographs of young men and young women and happy groups in city squares, alpine villages, hotel balconies and spas, outside palaces, ruins, houses. It was a room of European mementos, but it was also a sick room, and this time I could see evidence of Lilli's devotion to her duties. Miss Dalgleish was neat and clean, her bed was smooth and white, the bedpans were under the bed, the medicines were neatly at hand, and the room was in perfect order. On a table near the bed were half a dozen books and the gramophone, and near it the chair that Lilli obviously used when she read or worked the gramophone. Near the door was the spare bed where Lilli slept—neat, white, pristine.

'Two of a kind,' I said to myself, seeing them together.

When I stood close enough to Miss Dalgleish to see her properly I was saddened to see how thin and wasted she was. Her face was skeletal, her eyes large. Lilli had braided her hair into a little top knot, and this made her face even more cadaverous. But her mouth was thin and firm.

'Good evening, Kit. Good evening, Mr Devlin,' she said.

We said good evening, but the effort of talking seemed to exhaust Miss Dalgleish. She watched Lilli, not us, and Lilli was obviously deciding how we should lift her.

'Kit, can you lift her off the bed by yourself?' she said.

'I think so,' I said, but I whispered to Lilli: 'She looks awfully weak. What do you want to shift her for?'

'She wants it,' Lilli said sharply. I was not to argue.

'All right,' I said, and as Lilli pulled back the covers I bent over Miss Dalgleish and as gently as I could I put one arm under her shoulders and the other under her waist and began to lift. There was almost nothing to lift, and I could smell the peculiar odour of dried old skin and a dried old parchment body. What I felt in my hands were bone and cloth.

'Devlin, take the other side,' Lilli said.

I had lifted Miss Dalgleish out of the bed, and as Devlin tried to help me on the other side he got his hands tangled in the cotton nightgown and his feet mixed up with mine. Miss Dalgleish said 'No . . .' painfully as he gripped her in the wrong place.

'Go away,' Lilli said to Devlin. 'Leave it to Kit.'

I carried Miss Dalgleish out of the room and down the stairs as if she were a bundle of rags, but I wondered what she was remembering of her life as she watched this odd procession of myself, Devlin, Lilli and little three-fingered Jackie. In fact she watched only Lilli who went ahead of us, walking backwards to watch each step I took. When I put Miss Dalgleish down as gently as I could on the big leather couch in the library Lilli took the pillow from Jackie and held Miss Dalgleish's head up as we stretched her out.

'Mind her hips,' Lilli said.

She covered Miss Dalgleish quickly with a blanket, even though it was a hot night, and for a moment we all stood around the couch wondering what to do. Then Miss Dalgleish said in the very empty whisper that was left of her voice, 'Thank you. I'm quite all right.'

'You can go now,' Lilli said to us, and she told Jackie to lock the gate after us.

I think I knew as I left the house that Miss Dalgleish would not survive the night. I knew why she wanted to be in the library rather than in her bed. She wanted to die living, not dead. She wanted all the lights on, and she wanted above all to be left with Lilli and no one else. So it was no surprise to me when Dorothy Malone telephoned me next morning to tell me that Miss Dalgleish had died at 2 o'clock that morning.

# 23

IT WAS A BIG EVENT IN OUR TOWN. MISS DALGLEISH HAD ALWAYS been there, even when we didn't see much of her, and now she was gone. There was a lot of coming and going in preparation for the funeral: town officials, lawyers, doctors, undertakers. We watched them, and we soon realised that Lilli was still the authority in that house. She was the one who dealt with all the traffic in and out.

J. C. Strapp, the Dalgleish lawyer, had telephoned the Melbourne Dalgleishes on the Sunday, and two elderly men came up on the Monday train for the funeral on Tuesday. They called at the house, but they didn't stay there. They went across the river to the Eyres, who had been away but returned for the funeral. On the Tuesday morning when Mr Ransom's big Dodge hearse left the old house there was a long procession of cars, trucks, buggies and motorbikes which carried every important man and woman in the town: almost every doctor, lawyer, shire councillor, shopkeeper, publican, businessman and even big farmers from the Riverain, my own father, Mrs Royce the owner of our newspaper, and dozens of people who were quite unimportant but somehow had reason to follow the cortege.

And Lilli.

She rode in the sidecar of Devlin's motorbike. Dorothy told me that she had been offered a place in one of Mr Malone's cars but she had refused. I rode behind Devlin and when we reached the cemetery Dorothy Malone joined us. After a few moments we found ourselves standing together at the tail of the long queue of important mourners who followed the coffin to the grave. Lilli was not dressed in the black dress she had worn for her mother's funeral, she was dressed in a dark blue costume with white lace on it. And this time she looked healthy and robust, in fact almost too healthy for the occasion.

I suppose I was more interested in Lilli than the last rites for Miss Dalgleish because I didn't know what to expect of her. I remembered that feeling she had somehow given us at her mother's funeral — that it was nothing to do with any of us. She had cut us out of it. But this time she seemed almost uninterested. She didn't try to get near the grave, she didn't stand apart or aside. She held Dorothy's arm and stood between Dorothy and me and Devlin on the outskirts of the crowd where we could hear but not see the actual ceremony. Someone, I think it was Mr Strapp, had arranged for a piper to play a Scottish lament, and when Mr MacIntosh, the barber, dressed in full Scottish kilt and tartan, played his pibroch we could almost see those skirls and wheezes curling up like summer smoke over that dry old cemetery in the early evening air.

We only knew that the ceremony was over when the people in front of us began to move away. I turned to go, but Lilli held my arm.

'Wait a minute, Kit,' she said.

She kept a grip on my arm as well as on Dorothy's, and we simply stood there, the four of us, as the others dispersed. Some of the townspeople greeted Lilli: Dr Dixon, Mrs Royce, the Eyres and many others. They all looked at us curiously as we waited there without moving, and when they had all gone and we could finally see the grave-diggers filling in the deep hole, I was suddenly aware that Lilli's grip on me was a real one.

We heard the cars and the motorbikes and the buggies disperse down the sandy road, and by the time the last pat of the shovel had rounded off the top of Miss Dalgleish's grave we were the only people left.

'Take me over there, Kit,' she said to me, and letting go Dorothy's arm she walked very unsteadily with me around the little overgrown passageways to Miss Dalgleish's grave which was now covered in the sort of dry but exotic flowers that our hot summer gardens could grow.

'Now go away,' she said to me. 'I'll walk home.'

'It's two miles,' I said, 'and you don't seem to be too good.'

'I'm perfectly all right,' she said. 'Just go, Kit, and take the others with you.'

'All right,' I said as she gave me a little push.

When I told Dorothy and Devlin that Lilli wanted to be left there they wanted to wait, but I said it was better to do what Lilli wanted, so we walked slowly back to the old picket gate and turned around to look at her.

Lilli was now on her knees, or rather she was simply sitting back on her heels like a child who has settled down to listen and to wait, and I remembered the day she had sat like that to listen like a pagan to the tomato plants closing up for the night in Mr Hislop's field. I couldn't see her face, and though she looked perfectly relaxed I knew that Lilli was now left with Miss Dalgleish as she had always been left with her—when there was no one to see or hear or know what was between them. And I knew it was certainly not for us to interfere.

'Poor Lilli,' Dorothy said, in tears now. She wanted to go back to Lilli.

'No. Kit's right,' Devlin said. 'Better leave her. She'll be all right.'

'But it's awful,' Dorothy said.

'Come on,' I said to Dorothy, and taking her arm we left the place on Devlin's rattletrap motorbike as if we had suddenly become intruders and must politely fade away.

We hadn't gone far—we were turning the corner at the end of the racecourse—when we were flagged down by Jackie and Tilley.

'Where's Lilli?' he said when he saw Dorothy in the sidecar.

'She's coming,' Dorothy told him.

'What's the matter with her?'

'Nothing. She's coming later,' I said. 'Get up behind me.'

Jackie climbed up over the back wheel and gripped me around the waist, and Tilley leapt into the sidecar with Dorothy as Devlin plunged forward in first gear. He took

Dorothy home, he took Jackie home (to Miss Dalgleish's), and he took me home, and when I got off the bike I said to him: 'What do you think will happen to Lilli now, Dev? What will she do?'

'I honestly don't know, Kit,' he said. 'And I don't think she knows herself.'

# 24

In fact Lilli simply went on living in the old house as if she was now a continuation of Miss Dalgleish. Which was what Miss Dalgleish had obviously planned and intended.

When Miss Dalgleish's Will was made public by Mr Strapp, she had left the house and its contents in a limited trust to Lilli, with a generous fund to provide for her during her lifetime. There was, however, a proviso that Lilli must live permanently in the house and maintain it. There were other bequests to the gardener and to Mrs Peters, but a niece in London was named as the alternative beneficiary if Lilli failed to fulfill the terms of the Will. A codicil had been added saying that there would be no objection in the terms of the Will to Lilli's brother 'John' remaining with her in the house, but The Point had to be sold.

I laughed when my father told us over dinner what the terms of the Will were. 'So she wins after all,' I said.

'Who wins?' my father asked. 'What are you talking about?'

'Miss Dalgleish,' I said. 'Lilli will end up being another Miss Dalgleish. It's exactly what the old lady wanted.'

'Nonsense,' my mother said. 'Lilli is very lucky. In fact it's incredible, considering where the girl came from.'

'That's the point,' I said, and because I could never explain Lilli to them I didn't try.

I know of no one else in the town who didn't think Lilli incredibly lucky, including Dorothy Malone, who felt nonetheless that Lilli was finally getting something she deserved — thanks to Miss Dalgleish. But I knew there was something here that was far more complicated than it seemed and I was not surprised when only a week later Dorothy came to our house on Sunday morning looking a little stunned and said: 'Lilli's gone, Kit. They've all gone. Even Devlin.'

'Where to?' I said.

'I don't know,' Dorothy replied. 'They just went.'

'Didn't she tell you anything?'

'Nothing. Absolutely nothing. She came to see me last night when they were leaving, but she wouldn't tell me anything except that she was taking nothing belonging to Miss Dalgleish except that black notebook Miss Dalgleish used to write in. She gave me this to give to you.'

It was a brown envelope, and in it was the black exercise book that Lilli had kept her own fragmentary notes in. Inside it was a letter written in Lilli's big childish hand which said: 'Dear Kit. I thought you might like this because you are the only one who knows anything about me, except Dorothy. When you have finished reading it, burn it. Lilli.'

'Why did she do it, Kit?' Dorothy said, and Dorothy was in tears. 'Why would she go off like that?'

'It's that old thing with Miss Dalgleish,' I told her.

'But Miss Dalgleish is dead.'

'Not to Lilli,' I said.

'But that's absurd.'

'Maybe . . .'

In fact when they heard of it most of the town thought it was a typical example of Lilli's kind of ingratitude—a tragedy in fact. Lilli had been left a fortune and a house. Miss Dalgleish had taken care of her to the very end. What in heaven's name gave Lilli the right to turn her back on it?

Perhaps nobody could answer that except me, and I knew that Lilli could do nothing else. Lilli had lived all her life on the very edge of an aberration—the kind that comes with gratitude and servitude. If Lilli had made another one of her sudden choices it was the choice she had been forced to make all her life. It was the choice she had always had to make with Miss Dalgleish, and she had made it again. She was Lilli Stubeck or she was nobody, and though many people thought her behaviour a natural reversion to the gypsy in her, I knew it was rather a reversion to something indestructible in Lilli that had kept her on her feet when so often, particularly with Miss Dalgleish, she should have been on her knees.

The curious thing is that nobody seemed very surprised that Devlin had gone with her. He had always been an oddity, so this was just another joke. Devlin had gone as he had come, and he had taken his Utopia and Lilli and three-fingered Jackie and Tilley with him. Where to? It didn't matter. He had left a big wooden box at the station to be delivered to the railway station at Bendigo, which didn't tell us much.

In fact all three simply disappeared off the face of the earth as far as we were concerned, and within six months Miss Dalgleish's house was stripped of its contents by her niece and the house sold to Mrs Royce who thereafter lived in it. I saw Dorothy a year later, happy and perfect at last in her nun's habit, and though we asked each other if we had heard anything about Lilli and Devlin and Jackie, we knew there was no trace of them, and probably never would be.

'But I wonder how on earth they get on?' Dorothy said.

I had wondered about that myself: Devlin who believed in Utopia and Lilli who believed in no such thing. What could they possibly mean to each other? In fact it was simply a matter of understanding Lilli. Once she grasped the point of Devlin's Utopia it would be Lilli who showed him the way to get there—not by the Sermon on the Mount but by that other apostolic instruction written somewhere in Luke which says that he who has no sword, let him sell his garment to buy one. And if two swords happen to be handy, that is better still.

So I personally think of them as perfectly matched, and I am grateful to both because when Devlin left *The Sentinel* I was given the reporter's job in his place, and to end the story happily I have never looked back.

## ABOUT THE AUTHOR

James Aldridge was born in White Hills, Victoria and attended Swan Hill High School. He began his career as a copyboy and then worked in the Picture Library of the Melbourne *Sun*.

In 1938 he went to London and worked as a newspaperman on *The Daily Sketch*. During the war he became a war correspondent in Finland, Egypt and then the Soviet Union working for The Australian Newspaper Service, the North American Newspaper Alliance of New York and also for *Time* and *Life*.

James Aldridge's first novel was written during the war when he was a journalist. After the war he decided to leave regular journalism to have more time for his novels. He has lived in the United States, London and Europe, with one long visit home to Australia. His wife is Egyptian and they have two sons.

James Aldridge has written twenty-two novels, many of them set in Australia. He is probably best known in Australia for *A Sporting Proposition* which was made into a film with a new title *Ride a Wild Pony*.

Some other titles in this series

*The Pigman's Legacy*
Paul Zindel

Consumed with guilt and grief since the death of Mr Pignati, John and Lorraine determine to help another old man they find in his abandoned house. They force their way into his life, full of plans to make amends for their past mistakes, but things go very wrong and they begin to wonder if the Pigman's legacy is simply too much for them to handle.

*Displaced Person*
Lee Harding

Life is ordinary for seventeen-year-old Graeme Drury until inexplicably, people start to ignore him. Gradually, his world slips away from him; and it becomes grey, silent and insubstantial. Graeme has to question what is real. Even his girl Annette, becomes a ghost. Alone he must come to terms with a new existence, moving in a dream that is horrifyingly true.

*Empty World*
John Christopher

Neil Miller is alone after the death of his family in an accident. So when a virulent plague sweeps across the world, dealing death to all it touches, Neil has a double battle for survival: not just for the physical necessities of life, but with the subtle pressure of fear and loneliness.

*Tulku*
Peter Dickinson

Escape from massacre, journey through bandit lands, encounters with strange Tibetan powers – and beneath the adventures are layers of idea and insight. Winner of both the Carnegie and Whitbread Awards for 1979.

*Survival*
Russell Evans

High tension adventure of a Russian political prisoner on the run in the midst of an Arctic winter.

*Mischling, Second Degree*
Ilse Koehn

Ilse was a Mischling, a child of mixed race – a dangerous birthright in Nazi Germany. The perils of an outsider in the Hitler Youth and in girls' military camps make this a vivid and fascinating true story.

*A Long Way To Go*
Marjorie Darke

The fighting rages in France, and posters all over London demand that young men should join up. But Luke has other feelings – feelings that are bound to bring great trouble on him and the family. Because nobody has much sympathy for a conscientious objector – perhaps the only answer is to go on the run.